Underleveled

J.J. Howell

Copyright © 2025 JJ Howell, Underleveled Entertainment, and Caffeinated Terrier Press

All rights reserved.

The characters and events portrayed in this book are fictitious. Any similarity to real persons, living or dead, is coincidental and not intended by the author.

No portion of this book may be reproduced in any form without written permission from the publisher or author, except as permitted by U.S. copyright law.

No part of this book may be used or reproduced in any manner for the purpose of training artificial intelligence technologies or systems.

ISBN (Paperback): 978-1967326006

ISBN (Hardcover): 978-1967326105

Cover design by Ino.

Contents

AUTHOR'S NOTE	1
PROLOGUE	3
1. WHO AM I?	6
2. WHERE AM I?	11
3. WHAT IS THAT?	17
4. WHERE DID YOU COME FROM?	23
5. YOU'VE GOT TO BE KIDDING ME	29
INTERLUDE	36
6. WHAT IN THE NAME OF THE TRIAD IS THAT?	37
7. MY, WHAT BIG TEETH YOU HAVE	43
8. ARE WE THERE YET?	51
9. ARE THEY GOING TO EAT ME?	58
10. IN THE LAND OF THE BLIND	67
11. WE'RE GONNA NEED A MONTAGE	73
12. IS SOMEONE CUTTING ONIONS?	78

13.	ARE WE THERE YET?	84
14.	DELVING IS FOR THE BIRDS	90
15.	SECRETS UNKNOWN	97
16.	WE KINDA NEEDED THAT	105
INTERLUDE		113
17.	THAT'S A LOT OF TEETH	115
18.	THAT WILL NEVER WORK	120
19.	THE LION'S PAW	125
20.	AN UNLIKELY BUFFET	131
21.	"HIRED" HELP	137
22.	THERE ARE TWO OF THEM?!	143
23.	REST HERE, WEARY TRAVELER	152
24.	A COWARD'S DILEMMA	158
25.	MIRROR IMAGES	164
26.	A BIT OF "SELF" LOATHING	170
27.	PROMISES, PROMISES	177
28.	THIS IS NOT WHAT I EXPECTED	182
29.	GOOD, BAD, I'M THE GUY WITH THE DINOSAUR	187
30.	THE WINDS OF CHANGE	195
31.	LOOTING THE ROOM	202
EPILOGUE		207

ACKNOWLEDGEMENTS 212

AUTHOR'S NOTE

BEFORE ANYTHING ELSE, KIND reader, I ask for your forgiveness.

Underleveled is my 2025 entry in The Inkfort Publishing Derby, an annual contest for independent authors to stretch their wings. We each rank 100 covers/titles and are then assigned one based on preference, in a randomly chosen order. There was no guarantee that I would receive one of my top choices, but thankfully Underleveled was in my top five.

As a "no spend" event, this book is as edited as I can make it in a reasonable amount of time, given that it is written and produced in a matter of months with only my own meager talents. It is a labor of love, and vague insanity.

I hope you enjoy it for the romp it was intended to be.

If you are interested in learning more about Inkfort Press Publishing Derby, please visit them here: https://2025pubderby.carrd.co/

I would also like to give an approving nod, and proper attribution to the free TTRPG: TinyD10. I spent quite a bit of time using the TinyD10 system to build character sheets and keep track of "skill points" and "spell slots" as well as "levels." While this is not a LitRPG book, it is a light progression fantasy that needed a back bone.

If you want to use their system for free, check them out here: https://td10.org/home it is licensed under Creative Commons

Attribution-ShareAlike 4.0 International (CC BY-SA 4.0), Copyright 2025.

PROLOGUE
SIGNS AND PORTENTS

Mason gazed lovingly at his son as he entwined his fingers with his wife's. The stonecutter had prayed to the Maiden, Linath for a boy, and the goddesses had delivered. Ten fingers, ten toes, and already sleeping well, thank the Mother, Svatha. He had lived the requisite six months before the naming ceremony could be held, to tell Mason and Astrid the child's fate. The baby, cooing peacefully in the straw basket, stared with large eyes at everything around them, not knowing the momentous occasion he was part of.

Alveth, Mayfair village's priest of the Crone, Egreth, stood solemnly before the three of them. His arms were raised and his head tilted back as he mouthed the words of the ancient ritual. Mason couldn't help but glance around the town square at his friends and family, considering how lucky they were to have settled in a Labyrinth town. The trade was brisk with newcomers frequently arriving and needing his services to establish their transplanted lives. He was more than happy to oblige, even if half the seekers' houses would be sold in the coming months when they didn't return from their sojourns.

The priest's chanting rose in volume and broke Mason's reverie. "We stand before you, Egreth, harbinger of fate, to bless this child..." Alveth cracked one eye open and glared pointedly at Mason.

"Oh, uh, Rolph," Mason muttered.

"Rolph," Alveth repeated. "May he know only prosperity and strength." He made a complicated sign in the air above the basket, Rolph following his fingers with interested eyes.

Alveth held out an expectant hand. Astrid stepped forward and placed a small blue crystal in his hand. Astrid had spent a night's vigil before the gates of the Labyrinth, kneeling in prayer, to receive the token for Rolph's naming ceremony.

The priest raised his hands high, sunlight glinting off the sharp facets of the gem. He spoke arcane words Mason had no understanding of, but they exuded power. Eventually, he continued in the common tongue once more. "Now we ask for the goddesses' blessing for this young man, to learn his fate should he step foot within the realm of the mighty."

Alveth held the stone to his mouth and whispered as he knelt in front of Rolph. A glow grew from within it, shining over the boy's face. The old man extended his hand and placed the gem upon the baby's forehead, and Rolph made his first sound since the ceremony started. Mason had hoped for a squeal of laughter but was unsurprised at the concerned tone erupting from the babe.

The cobalt glow suffused Rolph's features, and he calmed, staring blankly into the distance as the crystal dissolved into a thousand motes of light. Alveth's eyes were wide and white, lost in a haze of prophecy from Egreth herself. Mason waited with bated breath until Alveth started and stumbled backward, landing hard on his rump.

Mason ran the few steps between them to help the high priest to his feet again. "What is it, Alveth? What did you see?"

Alveth cast his eyes down, unwilling to meet Mason's gaze which the stonecutter did not take as a good sign. "Mason..."

"Spit it out, man," Mason demanded. He glanced back at his wife to find Astrid's cheeks streaked with tears. *Damnable priests,* he thought.

Alveth's mouth split in a soft grin as he dusted off his robes. "Rolph will have a happy life—"

"That's good—" Mason cut in, but Alveth hadn't finished his pronouncement.

"Provided he doesn't set foot in the Labyrinth."

Astrid's voice was soft, the question almost inaudible. "Never?"

"Surely you don't mean *never*," Mason echoed. The Labyrinth was a dangerous place. Many who entered didn't return, but they were often the overly confident and foolhardy types: those who attempted to go farther than their skills and talents allowed. Even still, to be kept from the Labyrinth's depths limited the child's career paths significantly. While dangerous, labyrinth delving was a pivotal foundation to Mayfair's economy. Still, no amount of preparation prevented accidents, either, and Svatha knew they had seen their fair share in Mayfair.

Alveth's gaze turned from comforting to steely in an instant. "I do not question the soundness of your bricks, do I stonecutter?" He gathered the hem of his ceremonial garb and stormed off. Mason knew at once he had overstepped, but it was too late. He would have to make amends before the next service.

Astrid's hand came to rest lightly on his shoulder from behind and he placed his palm over it, squeezing gently before turning to embrace her. "Ah, Astrid, there are worse things than a home-bound lad."

She nodded, sniffling. "He will have a happy life, at least."

"It will have to be enough," Mason said, but couldn't shake the sinking feeling in his gut.

Chapter One

WHO AM I?

Rolph, a man of *little* consequence, wanted nothing more than to be a man of *no* consequence in this exact moment. The thin woman who had entered his shop towered above him, her fists white knuckled and her face swathed in bright red rage. "I'd commissioned three window frames for my businesses, young man. Three. Far more than I would normally venture with your generous lack of skill, but I owe some of my business to your dear parents." Rolph mumbled a thank you, but it had scarcely trembled from his lips when she continued her rant. "And what do I get for my money?"

"Three window frames?" He offered helpfully then sneezed violently. He wiped his nose on a soggy handkerchief from his pocket. "Apologies. My allergies this time of year are awful."

She eyed him distastefully before grumbling and turning to the large package her manservant had carried in. "Would you call *these* window frames? Much less, would you even dare to call them window frames I would design to install in my buildings?"

So, they weren't the *best* of Rolph's work. The sharp arches were functional, ready to accept a glazer's panes, but held none of the gentle artistry his father had tried to teach him. And worse, he had genuinely been proud of these pieces. Certainly, his skills were not like his father's. Rolph had never been known to be a particularly talented stonemason. He'd done alright work with walls, but when it came down to the detailing chisel and less spreading mortar, his talent was strictly nonexistent—his clients' more positive critiques of his functional but soulless constructions notwithstanding.

"I'd like to refund you your money," Rolph chewed out bitterly. The cost of the materials alone might keep him from paying his Labyrinth taxes for the next month. He would have to scrounge another way to pay them off.

The businesses and homes clustered around the gates of the Labyrinth were required to pay a fee for general insurance purposes. Sometimes an adventurer might accidentally let a low-level monster out past the gates to wreak minor havoc in town, or the tremors caused by a deep-level boss raid might break glass or damage belongings. Without it, Rolph's stonemasonry may be determined to be a liability and could be shut down permanently.

Reva Magnusdottir inhaled deeply, her anger abating at his pitiful offering. "Look, Rolph. It's been six years since you took over this place. Isn't it time you considered whether you're suited to this profession?"

As if the question didn't keep him up at night on the regular already.

He thought of his father, and of his mother. The powerful dynamic duo who had raised him. They were generally beloved by their community, the church's animosity excluded. His mother's touch with pack animals lent itself to the adventurers who descended into the Labyrinth; and his father, whose stone craft spoke volumes for itself. He often wondered about the last letter he'd sent them, in their state of blissful retirement. Did they believe the lies he'd written? Yes, the business was in good hands. Except it wasn't. Of course he was successful... at being late on his bills. Moreover, did they believe his lie that he was happy?

He reimbursed the customer and closed up shop. Not that he had other patrons to meet with that day, but it was the principle of the matter. He needed to sit with his accounts and make a plan and have a chance to lick his wounds.

Once the door was locked, and the lights were out, he descended into the basement where he kept his small living space. The basement wasn't meant to be anything more than a storage space, or a workshop. The family normally lived a few streets away, preferring their place of business as a separate entity from their comfort. However, once his parents had left him in charge of the shop, he could no longer afford the old family home in addition to the business. He'd told his parents it was so he could spend more time working on his commissions. In reality, he had sold it to pay off the invoices that had towered over him.

A small cot had been shoved between two walls with just enough room to crawl into it from the foot, and his laundry hung over the rungs of the rafters. Amidst the tools on his work table were scattered late payment notices and well-worn self-help books. Worthless heaps of intention which had thus far produced nothing of merit.

Rolph had tried everything he could possibly try and came up short handed. In a world filled with people who could do things, anything, Rolph had been dealt the worst of cards: he was talentless.

A skitter in the corner and a squeak pulled Rolph from his bitter musings. A small blue mouse had appeared on his table, preening up at him. "Hey, bud," he muttered and lowered himself heavily onto a stool. He extended his hand, and the mouse tip-tapped onto his palm, tiny feet barely weighing against his skin. The mouse rubbed against his chin, and he smiled. "I hope your day was better than mine."

Astrid, his mother, was a renowned animal speaker. Not true speech, but animals trusted her, and it was almost as if they shared a language of gestures and tone. Her training and aid were highly sought after. She specialized in medium-sized creatures like horses, donkeys, bears, and large cats.

Rolph, on the other hand, could only "speak" to small creatures such as these. Unless adventurers heading into the Labyrinth needed a mouse or a lark for their business, Rolph's abilities were, for lack of any better term, useless. And so it went.

Mason and Astrid had tried anything they could for young Rolph. As a child, they put his hands into the church's cold, holy water the way arcane summoners did for their children to ascertain magical affinity; and found nothing. They brought him by friends' places of business: clothiers, cobblers, cooks, woodworkers, and even the blacksmith, all to no avail. Eventually, they judged his regular comfort with stonemasonry tools were passable enough to place him in the mundane trade.

Astrid had found him one evening talking with the sparrows in the backyard when he was fifteen and had taken him to meet beasts of burden in the stables. Rolph couldn't seem to find the same rapport he showed with the smaller creatures. It had been the first time in his life he'd felt he'd disappointed his mother, even if she never showed it.

If his parents were anything, they were loving.

Which made the failing family business even harder to stomach.

The mouse nuzzled into his chin and chirped. Rolph repositioned him on his shoulder and stood. "Better find us something to eat, shall we?" He asked the small creature. He'd built something akin to a larder in the corner opposite his bed, and he navigated to it, balancing the mouse carefully as he went. In addition to the small space filled with a house's load of furniture and mementos stacked high, there were a few floorboards now and again that were in steady, rotting decline.

He rummaged around for some cheese, which he broke into small finger sized pieces and shared with his new friend.

He needed groceries, and soon. But buying groceries would mean he wouldn't be able to pay the invoice for the limestone he'd purchased. Maybe he could clean up some of the furniture he'd stowed away to sell.

His thoughts were interrupted by a sudden rumbling that filled the air, and the world pitched around him. His hands shot out to anchor himself on a stack of overloaded bookshelves. The mouse squeaked its indignance and leapt from his shoulder, scampering away from Rolph's vision. He clung tightly to his anchor as the quakes rippled through the building. Astrid's coveted dishes splintered onto the floor with a great crash, and his recently purchased slabs cracked along the work table. His tools flew akimbo in a great cacophony of chaos.

After a few moments, the world stilled, and Rolph beheld the enormity of the mess that had been his life.

He inhaled once, twice, and steadied himself on the larder. "At least I paid this month's Labyrinth tax," he muttered aloud, and took a step forward to begin his clean up.

Only, instead of finding a solid wooden board beneath his foot, he fell into the darkness below.

Chapter Two

WHERE AM I?

Rolph tumbled and twisted along a dark tunnel. Every time he tried to get his feet under him, his momentum would carry him forward. The disorientation of the pitch blackness added to his confusion with each roll. Down might as well have been up, with his back and shoulders taking the brunt of every wall and rock he collided with.

Will. "Oof." *I.* "Ow." *Ever.* "Hurgh." *Stop falling*? He asked himself and slid in the dirt for an indeterminate amount of time before finally coming to a halt. Rolph lay there, panting, aching, and blind. No light emanated from any direction and he cursed his parentage for the first time in his life. Dwarves could see in the dark, but he had been cursed with human eyes.

He sat up slowly, gingerly prodding his arms and legs to determine whether anything had broken in the fall. Luck was not his usual companion but, other than tender spots that would surely turn into sizable bruises, he seemed to have suffered only minor injuries. What he would have given for a torch or even candle at that moment.

It took a long moment for the vertigo induced by the visual deprivation to subside and he could get to his feet without wobbling. His questing fingers found loosely packed dirt along the walls, and the air was full of detritus he had kicked up during his mad tumble. After more than one turn around, checking his environs with his limited senses, he found only two walls and a stretch of nothingness in either direction.

Rolph came to a terrible conclusion. "I'm lost," he whispered into the darkness. "I don't even know which direction I fell in..."

As he stumbled along the path, he kicked something hard which skittered audibly across the floor. His heart quickened and he froze, afraid he had disturbed some underground creature. Rolph waited, but nothing else happened, no sound or movement, so he knelt and crept forward sweeping the ground in front of him.

He started when his hand brushed something cool and solid, but he managed not to cry out. *Keep it together, Rolph*, he chided himself. Despite the tremor he couldn't see, but knew was there, he reached out again and closed his fingers around a long thin object. He sighed in relief as he recognized the wooden shaft of his favorite hammer. He pressed the cold steel of the wedge-end into his hand, checking to make sure nothing had broken.

He let out a small chuckle which echoed strangely as he tucked the tool into his belt. *I'm lucky it didn't land on my head on the way down.*

As he knelt there, the dust settled around him and the air tasted less like the floor of the shop after a long day of work. Time hadn't improved his sight, and no glow emanated from either direction. He reached into his pocket and took out his last copper. Rolph had planned to drown his sorrows at the pub. One or two coppers wouldn't have saved him from bankruptcy so what could a drink have hurt? He rubbed the coin between his fingers so that he could feel the familiar imprint press into his fingers. Svatha's stylized face on one side, and the lion representing her fierce protectiveness on the other.

"The lion and I go forward; the Mother and I turn back. Not that I know what forward means right now anyway..." He flipped the coin higher than he had intended and grasped blindly to catch it, being rewarded with the thump of it hitting the ground. Rolph sighed and stooped to retrieve it, but the smallest breeze of fresh air drifted past his face. When he picked up the coin Rolph checked the face of it with his thumb to find the lion sitting proudly on top. "Onward it is."

Rolph made his way through the tunnel, first groping along the wall but later trailing his fingers lightly along it as he walked. The floor was surprisingly clear and sloped downward. It was dry, but he imagined for a terrifying moment it might fill with water, and he would be washed away along with the rest of the litter. Rolph swallowed the thought where it sat heavy in his stomach.

He walked for hours, or so he imagined. Sometimes he would get turned around, other times encountered dead ends and even fell short distances as he descended. He often stopped to regain his bearings, waiting until he sensed the current of air. Three more turns later, he was nearly blinded by a pinprick of light in the distance. Rolph said a prayer to the Mother and set off again at a run, tripping more than once in his haste to make the small glow blossom into a small, rough square, then finally resolve into a cave entrance.

He stumbled when he made it to the cave entrance, leaning roughly against the rock wall, waiting for his vision to adjust and his lungs to catch up with him. His knees and ankles were scraped and raw from his various falls, now that he could stop to examine them.

Where am I? He wondered, rubbing a sore spot on the side of his head.

The cavern beyond him had a high ceiling with clusters of lights hanging from large root systems penetrating through rock and dirt. They flickered bright yellow and blue, filling the space with a gentle, colorful brightness. While he might be able to see his hands and feet, it was still too dark for him to properly make out more of his surroundings. Hulking objects that his brain understood to be great rocks: stalagmites maybe? Boulders?

He was obviously underground.

"Okay," he muttered to himself, pushing back from the archway from which he'd emerged.

Before he got too far, an unnatural chill ran over his skin and shivered up his spine, and his mind ached as though it had struck a wall. He staggered momentarily, wondering if maybe he'd sustained a concussion somewhere in his initial fall. "I'm going to have to find a labyrinth barrister," he grumbled, rubbing at his forehead. Maybe the money from the insurance claim could save his shop, long enough to close it down, at least.

How was he going to get out of this one, anyways? After a few steps forward, he glanced back at the space he'd emerged from. It was nothing more than a collapsed animal warren, though the animal who made it had to have been massive. The idea of trying to climb back to the surface or find his way in that horrible darkness harrowed him. No, he would have to find another way out.

A growl and a scrape sounded from the distance; something large in the low light of the caverns, and realization dawned on Rolph.

The Labyrinth.

"Ugh," he grumbled as the wheels in his mind raced backwards.

The Labyrinth was the last place he was ever supposed to set foot in. He'd heard the story time and again from his parents. It didn't help that old Alveth gave him pitying eyes when he attended service at the church, or did odd jobs around the building. No one ever told him why, and over the years, the most Rolph dragged out of the priest was that he would meet a terrible end if he entered the depths.

"Maiden's tears," he mumbled under his breath in sudden understanding. Rolph likely *was* concussed, but the shiver that came over him entering the cave was nothing so natural as a bump on the head. When a delver entered the maze for the first time, the magic of the Triad changed them. Each person, based on their prior skills and talents, became something more than they had been before stepping inside.

Except Rolph hadn't used the main entrance. He had no way of knowing where in the Labyrinth he had entered, but based on the size of the abandoned burrow, he was much deeper than he wanted to be. Whatever abilities the goddesses bestowed upon him were a mystery, intentionally shrouded by their enigmatic magic. The entire Labyrinth was a test for the faithful and brave to prove themselves against the challenges of the Triad.

That being said, no one loved that kind of mystery. A whole economy had developed over the years, well before his parents settled in Mayfair. Labyrinth mentors, guides, trainers; it seemed like anyone who could comfortably survive the first layer put out a shingle to sell their services to the unwary newcomers. People would accost you as soon as you walked in, offering to divine your skills, magic, or other powers.

But Rolph had no such luck. If he could figure out where he had stumbled in, perhaps he could find his way through to the exit. Maps of certain layers existed, but they were almost entirely limited to the first five levels. The deeper you went, the less likely the survivors of those adventures shared their wisdom. Whether the discretion was due to greed and an unwillingness to share the secrets that made them rich and powerful, or simply a lack of desire to relive the traumatic events, no one could say.

"Well, this is a fine—" Rolph began to say but cut himself off as the scrape of something solid against stone echoed through the cavern. *I have got to stop talking aloud, it's going to get me killed,* Rolph chastised himself, but bad habits died hard.

He crouched low and ducked behind a stalagmite taller than him and closed his eyes, keeping his breath as shallow and quiet as possible while staying alert for additional movement. The noise came again, and this time it reminded him of horses' hooves as they sometimes scraped along cobblestones. Rolph hoped for a moment a stray pack animal might have found its way into the warren he found himself in, and he risked peering around the stone.

He didn't like what he found.

Chapter Three

WHAT IS THAT?

"Crone's beard!" he squeaked before clapping his hand over his mouth.

The creature clomping heavily not fifty feet from his hiding spot was no lost dray. It stopped in its tracks and raised a bovine snout to the air. The monster easily stood a head or more higher than him, though at a less-than-average five-foot-four, he had never been accused of being tall. Two cloven hooves graced the body of a bullish humanoid figure, black fur glistening in the glowing light of the bioluminescent lanterns.

Rolph had never laid eyes on a live minotaur before, though the rare delver who had traveled deep enough to encounter one had brought back a head for mounting. Despite what might have been a once-in-a-lifetime experience, Rolph quickly determined he would have given all his remaining worldly possessions to have avoided this very instance.

Maiden preserve me, Rolph thought in silent prayer as the monster turned in the direction of what he hoped was his still concealed gaze. The angry snort which emanated from its mouth told a different story. Rolph twisted behind the rock once more but the clatter of unshod hooves on stone rang out and the creature charged his position, the sound coming closer with each passing second.

The time for stealth had passed. "You have got to be kidding me!" Rolph cried as he lunged from his hiding spot just as a gargantuan hammer shattered his former cover into gravel. Rolph considered running for the dirt tunnel, but he guessed the minotaur would fit even if it was a tight squeeze. The thought of trying to outrun his assailant in complete darkness drove the option from his mind. Instead, he ran further into the cavern, weaving among the standing stones.

Rolph was no tactician, but he knew from the few times he had been chased by town dogs when he was younger that a charging animal needed a clear path.

CRASH.

He spared a look back and found the minotaur pursuing him in a relatively straight line, the stalagmites posing no problem for either its hammer or, perhaps more distressing, its horns. Rolph stopped his efforts at creating obstacles and focused instead on distance. His breath came in ragged gasps and sweat poured into his eyes. He was sure he had gotten far enough away when the hammer's head, as large as his chest, crashed down to his right. It narrowly missed his shoulder and threw him off his feet with the proximity of the impact to the ground.

Rolph rolled a few feet, then climbed dizzily to his feet. The minotaur ignored him, attempting to pull his hammer free from where it had struck, but an occlusion in the stone held it fast. The monster grunted and strained but paused to glare at Rolph when he raised his hands in surrender.

"I'm—" he coughed and sputtered, trying to regain his breath. "Not even supposed to be here. If you'll let me—" Rolph groaned in dismay as the minotaur set its hooves for another charge. He turned and ran, faster than he ever had in his life, but knew it wouldn't be enough.

In his mad dash, he almost missed the edge of a cliff, jutting out over a black expanse of nothing. He skidded to a stop, barely managing to not pitch himself over. Rolph turned with a sigh. He was no warrior, but if this was the fate Alveth had seen for him, he was going to face it in the end. Fatalistic adrenaline steadied him. He considered his assets, which were his hammer and, well, that was it.

"I'll make do with what I've got. I've done with less," he said, reaching to his belt to find...nothing. He pawed his waist, and the damnable thing hadn't slipped around the back. It was simply gone. No, there it was. He eyed the dull metal of the head laying in the dirt ten feet away, sitting between him and the charging minotaur.

In what was either the most heroic, or idiotic, moment of Rolph's life he ran *toward* the minotaur and lunged for the hammer. The creature's greater speed meant it reached the hammer before Rolph did, only it clearly wasn't paying attention to the tradesman's tool. It only had rageful eyes for Rolph, which led to the second most unlikely event of the day. The first being Rolph's sudden appearance in the labyrinth.

The second? Rolph bore witness as the minotaur, fully intent on his death, *tripped*. The monster's hoof hit the stonemason's hammer, and it stumbled, then tried to catch itself. Rolph had been mid-dive for the hammer and his body collided painfully with the minotaur's legs, fouling its footing even further. Its momentum carried it forward over Rolph's prone form, launching it into the air. The beast howled as it twisted mid-flight, then landed with a jarring crash. It tumbled once, twice, then disappeared over the edge of the cliff. The creature bellowed in outrage, though its volume faded from Rolph's hearing as it fell. It finally stopped with a muffled thud when, as Rolph could only assume, it hit whatever hard surface lay below.

The young man rolled onto his back, gasping for air and clutching his ribs. He had never broken one before, so didn't have the experience to know whether he had done so now. In contrast to the discomfort, warmth spread through his entire body and displaced the pain for a handspan of heartbeats. Was he developing a fever? The Triad only knew what kind of mold lived in the depths and he had been scraped raw in multiple places on his trip down the monster warren.

No, it wasn't likely he was falling ill, at least not this soon after entering the Labyrinth. The sensation radiated from the center of his chest through his extremities. Surely, he—the thought struck him as hard as the minotaur. Some delvers called it the "reward", the benefits reaped from killing monsters. Each death transferred a bit of magic to the victor, and in this surprising case, it was Rolph. He flexed his fingers and found them ever so slightly less sore. Sitting up, his ribs protested loudly, and he nearly fell over again. Clearly, whatever the minotaur's death had done for him wasn't healing his injuries, only making them feel more distant for the moment.

The brief respite let a new factor creep into his awareness, and another low growl echoed in the chamber. He rolled into a crouch, peering right and left until the sound came again. This time he pinpointed the source and laughed at himself, though he kept quieter than the last outburst that drew the monster to him.

When was the last time I ate? Rolph considered the timeline of events. On top of never making it to the pub to spend his last coin, he hadn't scrounged up dinner for himself after dealing with his last customer of the day. Another challenge made worse by not entering the right way. Despite not knowing which level he had rolled into, he made a fair assumption there were no handy merchants sitting around waiting to sell him a sausage roll.

His stomach gurgled louder at the thought. Rolph imagined the splattered minotaur and couldn't recall when he'd last had a good steak. Despite its relation to a bull, the humanoid aspect of the creature turned his stomach when he imagined it butchered into chops. No, he was unlikely to find anything delicious in this dungeon.

He eyed the giant war hammer still lodged in the stone floor some distance away, considering whether it would be worth trying to free it for either use or barter if he came upon another living soul. Rolph stood with a groan and made his way cautiously to where the weapon rested. The idea of taking it with him seemed less appealing the closer he got, until he stood beside the thing and shook his head. Without storage magic or an enchanted rucksack, there was no way he could expect to carry it any reasonable distance.

Still... he thought, placing his hands on the long handle.

He gave it one massive heave, his muscles straining, and yet the damned thing budged not a fraction. Squinting down at it, he reshuffled his feet for leverage, and *yanked* again, grunting this time in the effort. Nothing.

He looked about the edge and scuffed his foot along the breaks, hoping to knock the weapon loose, but it was still firmly stuck in the floor. He ran his fingers over the striations in the rock in the dim light, trying to judge what kind it might be. Maybe there was some way he could break it along a seam, setting the hammer free.

What was at one point in time a passing fancy had suddenly turned into a frustrating puzzle that needed solving. He lost himself in the task, using his stonemason's hammer and a bit of rock to tap along the ridge the war hammer had lodged itself into. *Tap, tap, tap.* Each small echo made him scan the limits of his vision for visitors. The distant roar of monsters didn't seem to dissuade him, as much as it slowed his attempts. As long as nothing approached, he allowed himself to be drawn into the work. His fingers worked furiously, grappling and scraping his nails to get some purchase, enough to wedge his hammer in...*Crack! Slam!*

With one final stroke of the chiseled end, the stone finally gave way, letting the massive hammer fall to its side. Rolph jumped a little at the sound as it echoed through the cavernous space. He froze, listening for any noise that might signal a monster might be coming to investigate. After thirty seconds, without so much as a hint of distant scuffling, he turned to the hammer and lifted.

As much as Rolph had convinced himself it was the stone that had held the war hammer captive, he wasn't stunned so much as disappointed when even his strongest haul could not budge the weapon from the floor. He sighed and set his hands upon his hips, fingering the stonemason's tool he'd fit back into his belt. "Well. That solves that, then," he muttered, forgetting the promise he had made to keep his thoughts to himself.

"Need a hand?"

Chapter Four
WHERE DID YOU COME FROM?

Rolph might as well have screamed; his yelp shattered what silence he'd insisted surrounded him. A tall man in steel armor had approached him in his distraction.

"How did you—" *Wait, another person? This deep?* Rolph's eyes lingered on the fascinating sword buckled to the man's hip. A proper delver. Rolph's luck might finally be looking up. "I mean. I suppose I could. Thank you."

The newcomer raised the visor of his helmet, revealing dark curls and friendly brown eyes, a charming smile brightened his face. Rolph wondered briefly if monsters could take on forms of friendly passersby and flinched when the swordsman reached down and plucked the war hammer from the ground. The man paused, weighing the hammer in his hand and obviously letting Rolph's nerves settle. "You okay there? Seem a bit jumpy."

Rolph inhaled deeply and nodded. "Jumpy *is* the word for it, I think."

The adventurer extended a gloved hand, swinging the hammer onto his shoulder as though it weighed nothing at all. "Ross. Champion of the Labyrinth."

A Champion? Rolph swallowed heavily, eyeing the stranger. The more time delvers spent completing the Triad's challenges, the more they would change. It took time and effort to become a proper Adventurer, and everyone entered the Labyrinth on a level playing field. If this man claimed to be a Champion, then he'd been here for some time or returned on multiple trips. Ross waggled his fingers and Rolph remembered his manners.

"Rolph." If there was one thing he knew he was good at, it was firm handshakes. It was the least he could learn from his father. He hesitated, waiting to see if the man noticed he hadn't given his own title, but Ross tilted his head expectantly, fingers still clasped around his wrist, and Rolph relented. He wondered briefly whether taking a shortcut to his current depth would change his initial bestowal from the Triad. "Um... How do I know what level I am?"

Ross's eyebrow rose, and he released Rolph. "Explorer then," he whistled low. "How did you end up down here? That's a death sentence."

Rolph's stomach curdled and his blood ran cold. "Where is... here, exactly?"

"We're on the ninety-fifth level." Ross's voice was unflinching, matter of fact, but Rolph hoped for a long half-beat that he would add "Joking! You should have seen your face!"

To Rolph's horror, Ross did no such thing and continued to stare at him with unadulterated awe. He gave the man a weak smile and splayed his fingers in a weak flourish. "Surprise?"

Ross shook his head in disbelief. "Let's get you someplace safe, friend." He clapped Rolph on the back. "My party and I have our camp set up nearby."

Rolph nodded eagerly. Safety in numbers, like he'd heard from the adventurers in the tavern. It made sense.

And so, he eagerly followed Ross through the caverns.

The swordsman insisted he hide behind the rock outcroppings when they encountered what he had called "low level mobs."

Some of which were the same minotaurs Rolph had struggled against, and otherwise consisted of giant, terrifying spiders and heavily equipped goblins. Sometimes, he gestured Rolph forward to deliver a final blow to the downed enemies. The same, bright, warm sensation filled his body after every kill and Ross nodded approvingly.

It took them about an hour to return to camp. He whistled three short notes as they rounded a final corner, slowing his pace until two notes responded to theirs. "Here we are," the swordsman said, pulling Rolph by the elbow around the bend and through a smaller cave entrance.

The light of lanterns lit the space dimly, but it was bright enough for Rolph to make out the features of Ross's party members.

It was a relatively small adventuring party, compared to what Rolph was used to seeing. Some of the parties he met in town consisted of anywhere between six and twelve members. In comparison, Ross's party was only five strong: a young looking elf with light hair and an embellished staff, a woman with dark ringlets and characteristic rogue's leather armor, a man with a massive spear that Rolph recalled as a "footman's lance", and a muscled dwarf wearing a large double bladed axe strapped to his back and little else. Ross himself rounded out their number.

"Who is this?" the elf squinted up at Rolph, an air of disdain in their voice.

Ross patted Rolph's back. "A surprise. A new Explorer, he must have fallen down this far."

The rogue's mouth turned down at this and she covered her ruby lips in abject horror. "Oh no! This far down?"

Ross nodded sagely, "Ran into him while scouting. He apparently fought a minotaur."

"Goodness," the lancer muttered. "That sounds terrifying, given your lack of experience."

Rolph rubbed his head self-consciously, his cheeks burning hot. There was no helping it, though. These *were* the circumstances he'd literally fallen into. "I suppose it is." An understatement.

"What happened?" the elf asked, face impassive. Not that it gave Rolph any pause, elves were difficult to read on the brightest of days. The elves were a quiet race from the Northern Wald, a few days' walk from Mayfair. They lived centuries longer than humans, so watched the rise and fall of civilization with an impassive eye unless something caught their interest.

"Oh, give him a moment," the rogue chastised the elf. "Let him sit. Do we have extra rations?"

"Of course," the lancer said, digging into his pack.

"Sit, sit!" Ross said, pushing Rolph closer into the circle of friends.

Rolph did so, between the lancer and Ross.

"This is Eliard." Ross indicated the lance-wielder. "Fern." He nodded to the elf who threw Rolph a thumbs-up. "And Rosalind." The rogue waved with her fingers. "The half-naked one is Skarn." Skarn only chuffed in response, eyeing Rolph like he was sizing up a chicken for dinner.

Once he was off his feet, his stomach renewed its protests at how empty it was. The gurgle was loud enough that the party gave a chorus of laughter, and they passed a bowl of hot gruel to him. He had never been a fan of the mush, but one spoonful and he declared loudly that it was the best thing he had ever tasted. And he believed it, too.

Rosalind slapped Fern on the shoulder. "Someone finally likes your cooking."

Rolph eyed the campsite and found no fire ring or any heat source beyond the lanterns he spied earlier. "How did you manage a warm meal?" He shoveled more porridge into his mouth and discovered it contained small bits of salted meat.

Fern smiled, elbowing Rosalind. "Cantrips are good for little else this deep. Heating a bowl is a simple enough task."

Rolph's hunger pangs abated as he tucked into the food and leaned back with a sigh after scraping the bowl clean. He'd have licked it, too, but thought it would be a poor impression to give to his hosts so he restrained himself.

"Now that you've had a chance to eat, Rolph, can you tell us how you got here?" Fern asked.

Rolph cleared his throat. Sharing his story was the least he could do after their kindness, and he related the short but harrowing tale. The party passed glances at various points as he spoke. When he finished, getting to the point where Ross found him liberating the minotaur's hammer from the stone, four sets of incredulous eyes stared back at him.

"Well." Rolph slapped his knees and stood. "I don't need to impose on your hospitality for much longer. If you'll outfit me with a few torches, I bet I could find my way back."

Eliard's gaze softened. "Wish it were so easy."

"What do you mean?" Rolph asked. "Surely I can make the attempt."

Ross shook his head, the mail aventail of his helmet scraping against his breastplate. "You can't go back that way. The Labyrinth won't allow it once you've set foot inside."

The gruel became a cold lump in Rolph's stomach. "What now?"

"Now?" Ross grinned and thumped Rolph on the back. "You come with us. Skarn is a pathfinder. By his reckoning we're a day's journey away from the exit. Two, if we're beset by more challenging monsters."

Hope blossomed in Rolph's chest. "You'd take me with you? Even though I'm of no use to anyone?"

"Everyone has something they contribute," Ross said. "You can help set up camp, cook if we're not surviving on dry rations, that sort of thing. For now, rest. We'll move on first thing in the morning."

Rolph glanced around the cavern, perpetually lit by the glowing orbs and moss. "I didn't know it was nighttime. By the Mother, I don't even know what day it is."

Rosalind tapped an odd circular protrusion on one of her leather bracers. "Days are mostly meaningless down here. But we keep to a schedule with these timekeepers. Everyone delving past the fifth level has one."

"Sleep deprivation is rough," Skarn's soft voice was at distinct odds with his barbaric appearance. "Get too tired and you'll end up in something's stomach. Best to stick to a schedule. If you ever venture back down here, I suggest you find one for yourself."

Rolph nodded and his head had grown heavier since the last time he moved. The day's events had finally caught up with him and his eyelids began to close of their own volition. "Speaking of getting sleepy, I don't know how much longer I can keep my eyes open."

His vision dimmed, though he could still make out the rest of the party grinning at him. They must have understood the stress he had been under. *No one would blame me for needing to rest*, he told himself.

Eliard had disappeared between blinks and reappeared in front of Rolph just as suddenly. He carried a bedroll, which he laid out in front of where Rolph sat. Rolph collapsed onto it gratefully and nearly startled fully alert when Fern laid a cloak across him like a blanket.

One more day, he thought. Despite the hardness of the stone floor, he drifted off to sleep with a smile on his face. He was going home.

Chapter Five
You've Got to Be Kidding Me

Rolph came groggily to consciousness, stuck halfway between the delightful dream he had been having and the uncomfortable crick in his neck from how his head lolled to one side. He stretched his arms above his head or at least tried to.

"What's going on?" he asked, even if it sounded to his ear more like "Wuz gong" given how thick his tongue was with sleep. He tried once more to raise his arms but couldn't do more than wiggle his shoulders. His eyes snapped open and the realization that he had been bound drove the remaining lethargy from his body. "Ross?"

A low chuckle sounded nearby. It was the swordman's voice, but it held a sinister undertone that hadn't been present before. "Good morning, *Explorer*."

Rolph craned his neck and scanned the area which was unchanged from the night before. The hustle and bustle of the party breaking camp filled the air with a variety of noise. "Why am I tied up?" he asked, and Ross looked over at him from where he packed his gear into a rucksack.

"Change of plans. Fern!" Ross bellowed. "Put our friend to sleep again, will you?"

Fern's soft footsteps echoed strangely from Rolph's place on the floor until they towered over him. They peered down at him but not with malice, only a hint of pity.

"Please," Rolph begged with a quaver in his voice. "You don't need to do whatever it is you're doing."

Fern gave a long-suffering sigh. "Not much other use for these low-level spells, anyway." They scraped a pinch of dust off the cavern floor and sprinkled it over Rolph while murmuring arcane words.

The waking world fled again as Rolph tumbled back into darkness.

The next time he came to, he had been laid unceremoniously over a rock like a sack of grain. He wriggled until he fell off, landed painfully on his side with an "oof", then rolled over in time for Fern's boots to come into view before everything went black.

Rolph had no way to know how much time passed between each moment of wakefulness, but eventually he awoke to a rhythmic swaying, as if he was slung over the back of a horse. He stayed quiet, not wanting to alert anyone to his newfound lucidity, and took in his surroundings.

First, and closest, was the hairy back of Skarn. The man wasn't nearly as odorous as Rolph might have expected, but it wasn't a pleasant scent to wake up to. A combination of aging sweat and leather he doubted he would ever forget. Rolph surreptitiously glanced beyond his hirsute mount.

The cavern was large enough now that the ceiling might as well have been a moonless night sky. The glowing lights which dotted the earlier caves were now fewer and farther between. Packed earth studded with stones passed below him, Skarn's boots making puffs of the dry stuff as they walked.

They were no longer in the caves he had fought the minotaur in, though he mentally berated himself for considering it to have *been* a fight at all. *This is how I die,* he told himself. *Carried to my death by the cousin of a mountain devil.* Rosalind came into view, and he hastily shut his eyes, but clearly not soon enough.

"He's awake again," she cried.

"It's fine, we're nearly there," Ross replied, and his voice came closer.

Rolph's head bounced gently along with Skarn's gait. Without the threat of a sleeping spell, he gave up the pretense entirely and lifted his head to seek out Ross's face. "Almost where?"

Ross grinned and it held the same malice he had noted before his enforced slumber. Without the promise of rescue, or hope of returning home, the glamour Rolph's mind had placed on the party's appearance faded. Ross's armor had seen hard use and was dented, scraped, rusting, even missing pieces. Where a cowl once flowed around his shoulders only a tattered scrap of fabric remained fastened to a dull ornament on his shoulder.

"You're going to help us get out of here," Ross said before passing out of sight in front of Skarn again.

Rolph's gaze swiveled to Rosalind and took in her appearance with new eyes. Her leathers were discolored, whether from water or blood Rolph would never know. Her eyes held a haunted aspect he had overlooked in their first meeting. She wore a brigandine gorget around her neck, but a giant set of claws had rended it partially apart leaving long gashes in the hide.

"What does he mean? You didn't have to tie me up. If there's something I can do, I *want* to help—"

"You'd volunteer to sacrifice yourself?" Rosalind asked. "How noble."

"That isn't—" Rolph spluttered.

"Besides, we're only doing to you what the Labyrinth would have done anyway."

Skarn laughed darkly and gave Rolph an extra hard thump over his shoulder on the next step.

"How do you know? I might survive, even on my own."

Rosalind grinned. "Eliard's a bit of a holy man, he divined you the moment you hit camp. The Triad must have it out for you. A worthless class for underground, a meager set of skills, and *one* spell? We're doing you a favor, putting you out of your misery."

Meager skills, one spell, worthless class? The words drifted through his head in a confused frenzy until—

He must never set foot in the Labyrinth.

The words struck his mind like lightning. Alveth must have seen this in his naming ceremony, the terrible fate that would befall him if he entered the trials. Rolph didn't even have a way to know what ridiculous "blessings" the Triad had stuck him with, or how to use them. No one was supposed to enter at the second level, let alone the ninety-fifth!

"What do you mean, sacrifice?" Rolph asked though his thoughts raced with anxiety.

Skarn's soft voice answered, vibrating his back against Rolph's stomach. "Someone needs to distract the guardian of the gate. They're not likely to survive, even Champions like us."

"We were going to draw straws, the night you showed up," Rosalind added. "You could say we're lucky you came along at all."

Rolph couldn't make sense of things. The guardian of the gate? What gate? And how would that help them get out of here? Did they mean to leave the Labyrinth? He had heard of some adventuring parties accidentally exploring farther than their equipment allowed and succumbing to the error of their ways. But to encounter one so deep as the ninety-fifth level? Labyrinth sickness must have set in with this party. They must be making some sort of mistake, or were out of their minds.

"There's got to be another way," he tried.

Eliard chuckled sardonically. There was a bitter and sad edge to his voice when he said, "You don't believe we haven't thought about this? We've considered the possibilities for a long time. We don't have enough supplies to wait for a better solution, we have no stones to teleport back to the surface. The only way out is through."

Ross tapped his forehead, dipping into Rolph's visual field with a taunting look about his handsome face. "See, at every gate, you have the option of returning home, instead of continuing on." His footsteps faltered and his face grew dark. "We've attempted to defeat this level several times now, but the guardian is too strong. You will distract the guardian so we can sneak past and activate the door. It's the only way we'll finally be free."

"It's been two years since I've seen my daughter." Eliard bemoaned, his voice thick with emotion.

Rolph's mouth hung open in disbelief. *Two years?*

Rosalind scoffed. "Stop whining," she told the cleric, and returned her awful gaze to Rolph. "So do the world one last favor and die, so we can make it home."

Rolph opened his mouth to protest again when Ross held up a hand, signaling the party to stop. They all listened carefully. Rolph couldn't hear anything, but saw the others' faces set in grim lines. Whatever it was they had heard was enough to set them on edge.

"Enough of this babble," Fern grumbled under their breath. They grabbed Rolph roughly by the hair, jerking his face around. They fit a bitter tasting cloth into his mouth and tied it tightly behind his head, gagging him. "Let's set him up and get into position."

Ross frowned and whispered back. "We're almost where we had decided on earlier."

Fern shook their head. "No, the guardian is obviously too close by. We'd catch our own deaths before we've even finished tying him up. We put him...*here*," they gestured to a dark rock outcropping, "and make our way around to the side. Once we hear the beast, we'll make a break for the gate."

"You're asking us to sprint two-thousand feet?" Ross argued. "Skarn wouldn't make it."

"I'll be fine," the dwarf shot back. "If it means I get to leave you wretched animals, my feet will carry me well enough."

Rosalind grinned. "If nothing else, if he falls behind, he'll give us a little more time."

Eliard let out a shuddering breath, nearly a sob. "Please, we've traveled this far together—"

Fern cut him off with a raise of their hand. "Enough. Yes, or no?"

"Yes," Rosalind and Ross said together, Skarn shrugged. Eliard nodded slowly. Rolph let out a bitter cry.

Ross and Skarn man-handled Rolph and shoved him up a small footpath worn into the stone over decades of dripping water. Rolph's feet slipped over the rock, but Ross's strong arms never faltered. Once at the top, they tied him with heavy rope with his back against a stalagmite. He could have made noise. It wasn't as though the gag silenced his groans, it only muffled words. Still, their sudden change in plans made him wary. Was the beast really nearby? If so, any extra noise or shouting might make for a quicker end than he had anticipated.

Once they were done tying him up, Ross removed his gag. "Scream all you like, it'll just draw the beast quicker." He patted Rolph's face. "Alright. It was great meeting you, kid. I hope it's a fast one."

Skarn nodded sagely. And then, the pair scrambled over the edge of the rock, disappearing and he was left alone.

Rolph tested his bonds once they were out of sight, pulling hard against his restraints, but they did not give. The sound of the party's scuffling below faded into nothingness, until the only sound was his own ragged breathing.

What now? He wondered, his brain sprinting through all of the fearful possibilities of what might be coming next. Was this the end for him? He didn't need to wait long before his answer came to him in the sounds of shaking earth and massive footsteps.

The guardian of the gate had arrived.

INTERLUDE

HUNGER

G'rtred's stomach growled. The scent of human sweat in the air made their mouth water. A distant clanging and scuffling of footsteps quickened their heartbeat. The delightful sound of panicked breathing would add spice to the hunt. There was also a tugging sensation in G'rtred's chest, a distant alert that something was approaching their door, their gate. That could wait. The tiny creatures' fear would keep the morsels at bay until they could eat their appetizer. Then, G'rtred could feast.

The little morsels had even left one of their own as an offering, tied up around a rock for G'rtred's imminent devouring. They had guarded the gate for longer than their memory existed and couldn't recall if that had been done before. The years had hardened their heart against the two-legged monsters that plagued the gate, but time had not made them cruel. The running-food would taste the best, perhaps the restrained one would make for a good pet.

Until the hunger grew again, that was.

Great gobs of saliva gathered at the edges of their mouth as they turned their large head and narrowed their sight on their prey.

Chapter Six

WHAT IN THE NAME OF THE TRIAD IS THAT?

Rolph squeezed his eyes shut and bits of an old parable echoed through his mind. *When the end of your days approaches...something something...face death head on.* He couldn't remember how the whole thing went, but it didn't matter. Rolph did *not* want to be courageous right now. He did not want to face his demise head on. He'd already done that with the minotaur, and it had placed him firmly here: with a worse fate than he could have imagined. He preferred being gored or thrown off of the cliff's edge over being double crossed by other people.

A low, chest-vibrating growl echoed through the cavern, raising the hair on the back of Rolph's neck. The scrape of scales against rock made it sound reptilian, and very, *very* large. The massive footsteps were evidence of that.

He sucked in a breath, trying desperately to stuff his panic down. *Is this how you want to die?* He asked himself. *You didn't charge a minotaur to be eaten with your eyes closed.* Rolph let out a long, slow, exhalation. In what he thought might be his last act of bravery, he cracked an eyelid open to behold what had come to slay him.

A great reptilian head swiveled in the air, far enough away from Rolph that he was certain he hadn't been spotted yet. The great beast inhaled deeply, as though searching. It stilled, then whipped in Rolph's direction. That was the moment the beast bared its teeth.

Rows and rows of dangerously sharp ivory flashed as the monster took another deep breath. Its entire body turned, and the stomping returned. The ground beneath Rolph shifted, and he would have fallen if his bonds weren't keeping him upright.

It was a dinosaur.

Specifically, it was a *Tyrannosaurus rex*.

Rolph had only seen drawings of them in books. The lethal predators were sighted in the very deepest levels of dungeons but once appeared throughout the world. The creatures had been hunted to near extinction, if Rolph remembered correctly. Seeing one in the flesh was a once-in-a-lifetime event, likely to be the last moment for any involved. Few people encountered a T-Rex and lived to tell the tale, if they managed to find one at all. His surprise was tempered by the reality of the Labyrinth. The Triad could do whatever they liked when it came to the trials, with the power of creation at their fingertips.

Rolph could have lived his entire life without coming within a thousand steps of a monster like this. And yet, here he was. Being sacrificed to one so the party could get away safely.

Crone's beard. If he had ever thought a day in the life of a skill-less stonemason was the worst, he had never been more wrong in his life. *This* was the worst day. And probably his last.

The dinosaur thundered closer, kicking aside great boulders underfoot like mere stones. Rolph could not tear his eyes from the creature. He tested his restraints once more, pulling as hard as he could, but it was still no use. He was going to die here, swallowed in one bite by the massive creature. Its head tilted back and it let out a roar that shook the entire cavern, blowing the hair from Rolph's forehead in a burst of air. He screamed. Why wouldn't he?

And then the dinosaur was there, its giant head cresting the edge of the vista, its hot breath burning against Rolph's face. If this was the vision the Church had seen for him, it was no wonder his parents kept him away from the dungeon.

"Wait!!" he yelled.

A tingling sensation tore through his body, and a blueish green glow emanated from his mouth. It shot up and curled around the dinosaur's snout.

As if in response to his desperate cry, the creature opened its mouth and bellowed in response. "ROOOOOOOARRRWHAT IS THIS?"

To Rolph's surprise, the beast stopped. Its large maw snapped shut and its head tilted.

"THE DINNER SPEAKS?"

To his ears the dinosaur was as loud as before, but instead of unintelligible growls the words rang clearly, echoing through the cavern.

"Yes! Yes!! I talk! Wait! Don't eat me!"

The dinosaur pulled its head back a bit further, regarding him with wide eyes.

"WHY DOES THE SUPPERLING SPEAK TO THE GUARDIAN OF THE DEPTHS?"

"I-I...don't know? I'm surprised you can understand me. A-Anyways, please! I've fallen down here, some people tied me up here for you. I hardly know where I am. I'm not supposed to be here!"

The T-Rex growled low. "YOU WERE ABANDONED?"

"Yes!" Rolph thought fast, hoping he could redirect the massive creature's attention. "A group of delvers kidnapped me. They're trying to sneak through your gate."

The dinosaur threw its head back and raged, no sound coming out besides unintelligible roars, then swung around and stomped in the direction it had come from. Rolph couldn't make out anything from his vantage point but soon the heavy footfalls of the giant lizard were joined by the screaming of humanoid voices.

Rolph winced at the crack of bones snapping under a heavy weight, quickly drowned out by another bellow from the T-Rex.

"No, please!" Ross's voice was an octave higher than his earlier bravado. "I just want to go—" His pleas cut off abruptly with a wet squelch.

Rolph had no tears to shed for the man, who had orchestrated his capture. A grim smile tugged at his lips despite the horror of the scene unfolding in shadows beyond the rise.

A deep gong sounded once, then twice. The tone of return echoed around and through him, signaling the departure of two of the party members. Perhaps Skarn had managed to run the distance like he had planned. Rolph waited, ears eager to know the fifth delver's fate, but nothing came. Eventually the dinosaur returned, coming into view again. Blood speckled its feet and snout, and it chewed lightly at something. The glint of metal, perhaps a belt buckle, peeked out from between its teeth before it swallowed heavily.

It approached Rolph's position again, though more cautious than before. The blue-green glow no longer limned its mouth, and when it opened its mouth as if to speak only terrifying growls came out.

Rolph closed his eyes once more, breathing deeply, and tried to tap into whatever he had done before when he begged for his life. He opened his eyes and concentrated on the dinosaur, focusing on the need to communicate, imagining them talking together like regular people did. A warm glow emanated from his chest and lungs, then pushed upward like an air bubble until it burst from his lips. He breathed out and the teal energy rose in a stream until it circled the beast's nostrils again.

He nearly wept with relief when the growls and rumblings turned to common speech once more. "ARE YOU BROKEN, LITTLE DINOSAUR?"

Little...it must think that since I can speak to it, I'm related somehow. Some T-Rex I'd make. Rolph chuckled though it caught in his throat and turned into a squeak. "Please," he said, coughing. "I'm trying to get back home. If I can get out of these ropes, I can climb out of here and go back the way I came."

The T-Rex snorted, its hot breath blowing Rolph's hair about like a summer wind. "THERE IS NO WAY UP, LITTLE SUPPERLING. THERE IS ONLY THROUGH." It tilted its head at Rolph.

Rolph's sweat had grown cold in the absence of the dinosaur's breath. "Can you untie me?" he asked. "Can you help me get home?"

"I AM NOT YET FULL, MORE THAN ONE WALKING FOOD ESCAPED." The dinosaur leaned in until Rolph's vision was eclipsed by one massive eyeball. "WHY SHOULD I LET YOU GO?"

Rolph quailed under the scrutiny but considered his options. This had gone better than he could have hoped for under the circumstances. He was alive, while most of the party who had put him on the chopping block were dead or gone. At this close range, Rolph could finally take in the finer details of his new captor. A handful of rough feathers dotted the creature's eye ridges. They weren't clean, or healthy, like a normal bird's, but drooping and dark.

"Are you okay?" Rolph blurted out before he could stop himself. "What happened to your feathers?"

The T-Rex turned its head away in a very human expression of shame. "I WAS CREATED IN THE LABYRINTH, BUT I KNOW WHAT THE SUN IS NONETHELESS. I AM NOT MADE FOR DARKNESS AND DANK CAVES BUT CANNOT LEAVE." The dinosaur rubbed an eye ridge against the edge of one stone, flaking bits of scale away.

"I'll take you with me," Rolph said, despite having no idea whether it was even possible. "If you let me leave, I'll bring you through the gate too."

The beast considered this for the space of seven breaths, large reptilian eyes narrowed upon him. Then, to Rolph's horror, its teeth flashed in a plunge towards him. He squeezed his eyes shut, expecting the pain of death to overtake him. He had tried, truly tried. He did all he could. He did his best all of his life, despite how insufficient it had been. None of the goddesses could ever suggest otherwise.

And yet, death didn't come.

The ropes fell from his body, having been severed by one great tooth, and the breath of the beast pulled away from him.

"COME, SUPPERLING."

Rolph gasped and dropped to his knees. Death had not come for him this day. Not yet anyway. "Where are we going?"

"OUT."

Chapter Seven
My, What Big Teeth You Have

Rolph scrambled after the Tyrannosaurus, doing his best to keep to the side so that he did not accidentally get caught beneath its gargantuan feet. His stomach did a massive flip when they passed the remains of some of the delvers. He recognized Ross's armor and Skarn's axe. Rolph didn't know if that meant the dwarf hadn't made it or had left his weapon behind in his haste. Either way, Rolph swallowed back bile and avoided looking too hard at the ground for the remainder of the walk.

When the gate came into view, Rolph's heart sank as he recognized his first mistake. The portal itself stood perhaps double the size of a normal door. While Rolph could have fit a small horse through, the guardian would never be able to cram its body through the doorway. Nerves settled in and he clasped his trembling hands together as he followed the dinosaur.

The T-Rex came up short and turned to Rolph, craning its neck down and huffing. Rolph's magic must have run out again. *I really need to figure out how this works*, he thought as he repeated his mental gymnastics again to reactivate the spell. The telltale glow suffused the T-Rex's jaws once more. *Maybe I'm actually getting the hang of this.*

"Sorry, I can only speak with you for short intervals. I'm not sure how long I can keep this up, either. I'm new to, well, everything I guess."

The dinosaur narrowed its eyes at him. "MAKE GOOD ON YOUR PROMISE."

Rolph gazed at the portal, which filled the doorway with a shimmering blue surface. An educated guess was the best he could manage, and he stepped forward. Apparently, his movements were too quick for the dinosaur's liking, and it growled. The sentiment required no translation.

He held his hands up in a placating gesture. "You're going to have to trust me, uh...what do I call you?"

"GERTRUDE."

Rolph had no idea whether that was her real name or simply what the magic had translated her growls into. His mouth hung open for a long moment before he clicked it shut. A small part of Rolph's mind recalled that in many species, the female was more dangerous than the male. Rather than reassure him of any motherly instincts, a cold sweat broke out across his back.

"Nice to meet you, Gertrude," he said. "I'm going to walk over to the portal, and I want to keep a hold of you. Can you swing your tail around? I'll try to bring us through, together."

Gertrude shifted heavily, and Rolph ducked as her tail sailed overhead to land next to the stone lintel. Rolph approached the doorway and laid a tentative hand on her tail. The scales were cool against his palm, much less rough than he expected. Gertrude let out a low rumble at his touch but didn't move away.

Rolph had no idea how the return gate worked, so did what anyone might do in his situation. He thought about home, placed his fingers against the azure surface that shone like solid glass, and closed his eyes.

After an embarrassingly long moment of silence, he took his hand back, then turned to stare at Gertrude. He was no master of reptilian expressions, but she seemed distinctly impatient.

"I—" His voice cracked, and he took a second to clear his throat and try again. "I don't know what I'm doing, if I'm being honest."

The glow faded from Gertrude's mouth, and her roar held no trace of the common tongue, yet Rolph knew exactly what she said. He briefly considered taking the portal home himself, leaving Gertrude behind, but a bright memory from his childhood rose in his mind.

"Do what you say you'll do," Mason had told him as he sat on a bench in the shop. "Your reputation is all you have."

Instead of making his escape, he focused on the small well of power within him and called up his one spell. This time, as the faint light danced along Gertrude's features, something within him was finally empty. *Well, that's the last time I'll be able to do that for some time, I gather.*

"I'm sorry, Gertrude. I promise I'll get you out of here, we just have to figure out how."

Gertrude's rumble was low in her chest, and she let out a morose: "AS YOU SAY, SUPPERLING."

Rolph pulled away from the gate and sat on a nearby rock. He felt Gertrude's eyes follow him with curiosity, but she didn't speak. "Is there some way we can condense you? Make you smaller?" He wondered aloud.

Gertrude bent at her legs so her maw hovered beside him. He wasn't accustomed to her hot breath and shuddered as a thrill raced up his spine. "I DO NOT WISH TO BE *SMALL*."

"Justtofityouthroughthedoor," Rolph rattled off as quickly as his lips could carry the words. He took a breath and slowed down. "Is there any other monster with a...pet? Minion? Something like that."

Gertrude tilted her head, considering. "THERE IS A BEAST THAT CARRIES A ROCK—" as Rolph's magic dissipated, her words turned into what he could only describe as a conversational growling.

She grunted at him, obviously annoyed.

"Right. Sorry." He rubbed his face tiredly. It had been such a terrifying day. "I won't be able to do that for a while," he told her. "Can you sort of understand me?"

Gertrude grunted. He wasn't sure if that was assent but powered on anyways. "If there's a beast that carries...I guess a necklace? We should just hunt him down."

When he looked up at the dinosaur, she only stared at him blankly.

"I guess you don't understand me as well as I thought you did," he sighed.

Suddenly, Gertrude's head whipped around at the sound of feet scrambling over rocks, and Rolph stood, startled.

Gertrude wasted no time in trampling toward the noise, just as Rolph caught sight of the robes of the person fleeing.

"Wait!" He yelled, running after Gertrude. "Gertrude! Maybe we can use him!"

The dinosaur didn't stop her rush toward the comparatively tiny human being. She nimbly scooped him up by his collar with her teeth. The man kicked and screamed, wriggling within her grasp. It was Eliard.

His screams were wordless, blood curdling things that made Rolph's ears hurt. Gertrude winced, and her large eyes looked at Rolph in a distinctly questioning manner. Rolph shook his head, and she rolled her large eyes. She couldn't eat him just yet.

Finally, the screaming abated, and Eliard heaved gasping breaths. His face was stained with tears that traced through the grime on his cheeks. His eyes were wide with panic and confusion.

"You're not dead yet," Rolph called up to him, taking great pleasure in the sway of the man's feet in the air.

"Y-You! How?!" Eliard babbled uselessly.

Rolph wasn't quite sure how, either, but Eliard didn't have to know that.

"Call off your beast!" the captive man demanded.

Gertrude huffed and Eliard yelped. She gave Rolph another pleading look.

"She's not mine, and she's pretty hungry." Rolph shrugged. "The only reason she hasn't eaten you yet is because you might prove useful to us." And maybe also because he'd probably soiled himself. Rolph didn't know whether that would actually deter Gertrude, but the thought of eating a chicken in its own refuse didn't sound appealing. Maybe he should make an effort to clean Gertrude's kills before she ate? *Listen to me, trying to mother a dinosaur.*

"I'll do anything!" Eliard cried. "Please, just let me down and we can talk like men—"

Rolph crossed his arms. "Did we talk like men when you put me to sleep? To be a sacrifice?"

Eliard couldn't get any paler. "That was a mistake! You're right, it was wrong of us. But it was Ross's plan, I never wanted to hurt you! Please, let's start over."

Of course he was begging Rolph. He rubbed his hands over his face. "I'll let you down if you can answer a simple question."

Gertrude grumbled, and her small hands curled and uncurled in a show of impatience. This was a waste of breath, he thought she wanted to tell him. Eliard sobbed at the sound. "Anything, please."

"Do you know of another guardian on this level? One with…" *Gertrude had said a rock. Was it a necklace? An amulet?* "Some sort of jewelry or rock around their neck?" He felt absurd asking but wanted clarity over sanity.

Gertrude blew a gust of air through her teeth, ruffling the man's hair. An encouragement, Rolph might say.

"I-I...There's a minor boss? He has a necklace like that! He walks along the western crevasse! P-Please, let me go! I just want to get home to my family!" He was crying again.

Gertrude's eyes looked at Rolph questioningly.

She didn't understand their tongue without magic, and apparently trusted Rolph to translate for her. The thought frightened him as much as it reassured him. He had promised to get her out of there, and at some point, they made the decision to become a team.

He turned his gaze to Eliard. "Tell me about the necklace."

"I don't know anything about it!" Eliard sobbed. "All I know is that he's hard to beat, a-and h-he has a pet? I don't know! Why do you want to know about it?"

"Have you seen him use the necklace?" Rolph pressed.

Eliard shook his head. "N-not direc—Please let me down! We can talk when I'm on the ground!" Gertrude was being polite with her teeth but couldn't keep the gobs of drool from sliding over her lips. Eliard whimpered as each droplet dripped stickily onto him.

The stone mason's son winced. "Alright." He muttered, mostly to himself, and looked around for something to bind the cleric with. He didn't want the man running off once he was set down. The area around them was a bare cavernous space, all rock and mineral. He jerked his head back toward where the adventurers had been trampled. Gertrude seemed to understand, following him as he retraced their steps to the tune of Eliard's desperate whimpering.

The sight of the remains of his captors didn't feel as liberating this time, and he had to stifle his roiling nausea with the back of his wrist as he dug through the belongings dropped in the chaos of...being eaten. He came up with some rope, a surprisingly unblemished backpack filled with rations, and Fern's staff.

He waved at Gertrude who lowered the cleric into his reach so he could bind the man's hands. "This is so you don't do anything funny."

Eliard nodded frantically, another glob of drool splatting onto his face. "I won't, I won't. I promise!"

When he had finished his knots Gertrude released her prey, straightened, and in an intimidating display, roared in Eliard's face. If Rolph hadn't been hanging onto Eliard's bindings, he reckoned the man might have bolted away. Instead, he stood with wild, terrorized eyes.

"Good. We've made our position abundantly clear. Tell us what you know."

"I don't know what to tell you, specifically? It's a necklace?"

"What does it look like?"

Eliard shrugged. "It's gray? Silver inset?" He shook his head, "I didn't get a good look at it," he admitted, looking tearfully up at the maw of the dinosaur. "Please don't let her eat me."

"Tell us more about this mini-boss," Rolph switched gears.

"Big?" Eliard's eyes were still locked on the flash of Gertrude's teeth. "Not as big as *that*. Four-legged, polearm wielder. Pet master?" He rattled off, as though they were listed on a paper.

"What's a pet master?"

Eliard's eyes returned to Rolph's for the first time since Gertrude had set him down. "You really are new, aren't you?" Rolph crossed his arms in answer, and Eliard continued. "They're monsters or adventurers who summon a beast companion to help them in combat."

"And the mini boss's pet?"

"He summons a cave crawler. He stores it in his necklace."

That was why Gertrude had mentioned him. Rolph nodded, recalling the insectoid monsters as a dangerous foe but nothing a Tyrannosaurus would have too much trouble with. He looked up at the dinosaur who watched him curiously. She couldn't understand the words they were saying, and he still couldn't muster the sensation to speak with her again. "Do you remember where he was?"

"Yes, I can—"

"Good, you'll take us there."

Eliard blanched. "Wait, n-no—I thought you were going to let me loose! Please, let me go home," his eyes filled with tears again.

Rolph shook his head. "You're the last person alive, as far as we know, that saw this boss." He nodded to the dinosaur still standing over the cleric. "So, there are only two ways you're leaving the Labyrinth. On your feet, after you guide us to the boss, or as a snack in her stomach."

Rolph jabbed a thumb in Gertrude's direction and, as if on cue, a dangerous growl emanated from her maw. He smiled to himself as the blood drained from Eliard's face again. It seemed like they were beginning to understand each other after all.

Chapter Eight

ARE WE THERE YET?

"A week's travel? You're kidding!" Rolph complained.

The one thing Eliard had not described, likely at least partially due to his terror of being eaten, was how far away their quarry was. Once his initial fear had passed, and an opportunity to clean himself off and change his undergarments, they had gathered a stone's throw from where the party had been trampled to set up camp for the night and prepare for their journey.

"If we're lucky," he replied. "The levels get larger the deeper you go. It also depends on what we encounter between here and there. The terrain varies and the mobs as well. No trip across the cavern system will be the same. There were times we barely made it, the five of us."

Rolph considered the journey, and their limited supplies. Food was covered for a time, the only slightly damaged pack of rations proved full of preserved meat, hardtack, and stale grains. He grimaced, considering that he must have been hungrier than he thought to enjoy his last meal of salted-meat porridge as much as he did.

A thought struck Rolph, and he had to give it voice. "You've been down here for two years? How did you have enough food?"

The grin Eliard turned on him was more than a little wild. "You think it was beef, what Fern fed you?"

A vision of the minotaur splattered against the floor of the cavern flashed through his mind and Rolph's stomach flip-flopped. The dried meat became immediately suspect, despite being the beggars in this situation. He swallowed hard, closing the pack for the moment.

Eliard's hard look softened at Rolph's discomfort. "It wasn't all scavenging. Some levels are more hospitable than others, you just happened to roll into a particularly stingy one."

"Well, we'll have to make do. Gertrude will have to hunt for herself." *Did Labyrinth monsters even need to eat?* he wondered to himself.

"I can also conjure a small amount of food and fresh water, periodically. It wasn't enough for a party of five, so it won't be enough for your friend here either. But we'll need to forage less for the two of us."

Rolph's survival skills were limited, but he knew enough to more thoroughly loot the bodies of the fallen party. His cursory inspection had netted him the food and staff, the latter of which he had no idea what to do with. A more diligent search, while pushing down his gorge as the corpses had begun to decay, earned him little more.

Ross's sword and armor wouldn't do him any good, but he found a plain gold ring on his pinky that seemed worth having. In addition to Fern's staff, he found a few torches and a small pouch full of vials. Most of them had shattered, staining the leather a darker shade of brown. Two had survived, however. One was deep red and Rolph recognized it as a healing potion. The other held an iridescent liquid which swirled in the light. He had no clue what it did.

He also found some completely mundane, if useful items. He started a fire with a flint and steel he recovered from one of Ross's pockets, made from scavenged, dry roots and scrub. In addition to the rations the supplies pack held a couple small travel kits for cooking and eating, dented pots and battered utensils. Rolph made a meager meal of oats, consciously stopping himself and skipping over the dried meat when his hand unconsciously tried to reach for it.

Eliard could manage to eat with his hands tied in front of him, so they passed whatever mealtime this was in silence. Rolph decided it was "dinner" based solely on his exhaustion. Gertrude seemed to agree and had lain down, a relatively constant scraping coming from where she squirmed against the stone floor. By the time they had finished their food, Rolph's eyes drooped half shut.

Eliard stared forlornly at his bonds. "You don't have to keep me tied up, you know? I'll get you to the boss, I promise."

Rolph's eyes snapped open, and he barked a laugh which echoed through the cavern. Gertrude cracked one eyelid at him and he grimaced, though that was not an expression she would likely have understood. "Forgive me if I don't trust you yet. You'll have to prove yourself and it sounds like we've got plenty of time for that."

In the end, Rolph tied one end of the rope to Gertrude's leg and set out a bedroll as far as the leash would allow. The dinosaur eyed him warily but allowed it. Rolph still let out a sigh of relief when he was done, thankful the beast accepted that a tiny thread was no threat to her. Worried about Eliard attempting to overpower him as he slept, Rolph set his own sleeping area on the other side of Gertrude's massive bulk.

The Labyrinth was no place for a good night's sleep, but Rolph's breathing evened and he was unconscious five seconds after his head touched the bedding. He slept for what might have been hours, or days, as time continued to be meaningless this far below ground. Eventually Rolph woke and stretched, muscles and joints popping loudly in protest for their inadequate cushioning.

Despite that, the young man stood with an energy he hadn't expected. His small internal reservoir of power had replenished itself as well. He would still have to be judicious with its use, but the fact that he would be able to talk to Gertrude again at least periodically comforted him.

Gertrude slept on, so he walked around her tail to check in on their erstwhile companion. His good mood fled when instead of Eliard coming into view, the untied end of his rope lay accusingly on the ground.

"Really?!" he yelled, which earned him a grumpy snort from his remaining party member. He hastily cast his spell and rounded on Gertrude.

"WHAT IS ALL THE NOISE, LITTLE ONE?" Gertrude grumbled.

"He's gone!" Rolph gestured wildly at where Eliard should have been, not even trying to conceal his panic.

Gertrude shifted her weight so she could examine her back leg and the subsequent lax rope. The growl that erupted from her was deep and guttural. She stood and whipped her body to and fro, searching in the dim light. She opened her mouth and sniffed the air and growled low. "WHERE HAS THE MORSEL LEFT TO?" She lowered an angry stare at Rolph. "WE SHOULD HAVE EATEN HIM, LITTLE DINOSAUR."

Rolph rubbed his head. He didn't know how good her sense of smell was but if she couldn't scent him, he must have put quite a bit of distance between himself and his captors.

And besides, how had he gotten out of the ropes anyways?

"I know," he muttered. "Maybe we *would* have been better off eating him." It was a half-hearted confession, one he meant solely for his partner. The thought of "we" eating Eliard turned his stomach. He would stick to his own rations. "Do you know where the mini boss we're looking for is?"

Gertrude let out a sharp exhalation. "IT HAS BEEN SEVERAL LIFETIMES SINCE I SAW HIM LAST."

Lifetimes? "What do you mean?" His eyes traced over the scars and patches of weak feathers molting over her skin.

"I DIE AND REAWAKEN HERE. IT IS A CYCLE." She snorted indignantly. "YOU WILL HELP ME ESCAPE IT."

Rolph winced. How many times had she been maimed or killed by delvers seeking the level's gate? How often did she face adventuring parties like Ross's: desperate to reach the surface?

He brushed off his pants. "Okay. It sounds like we still need Eliard. Let's find him."

Gertrude growled low but gave him a nod. "IF YOU SAY SO, SUPPERLING."

For the next half-hour, they scoured the immediate area. The spell, or whatever it was that Rolph used to speak with Gertrude, had worn off, but they were still able to communicate with gestures and, for Gertrude's part, grunts. There wasn't any fine sand, dust, or mud for footprints to lead them. Rolph eventually stumbled upon a loose hemp fiber that must have caught on Eliard from the rope. It gave them a general direction to follow, at least, and so they took it.

Gertrude kept pace with Rolph's much smaller legs, often having to stop and wait for him to catch up to her before she continued on her way. They walked in silence most of the first hour. Rolph wasn't sure she would even appreciate the noise of him talking without the spell. It wasn't like she'd understand him anyways—and he wanted to save his spells for when it was important. He could have used her during the interrogation the day before. He didn't want to make the same mistake twice.

An hour into their hunt, something caught Gertrude's eye. Or, it must have, because her whole body tensed. Her head whipped up, her mouth opening to taste the air, even as it rushed through her nostrils. She growled low, indicating to Rolph that she had found something. He scampered over the tall rocks between them and found what she had seen.

A bit of blood had dripped onto the stone floor, creating a trail they could follow. Other signs of a scuffle were present: white scrapes against the stone, a tear of fabric which looked similar to the black of Eliard's robes, and purple drops that had also dried alongside the red blood. There were also three arrows and a discarded dagger strewn haphazardly about.

Rolph frowned and cast his speaking spell. Teal magic spilled over his lips. "Who did this?"

Gertrude's eyes were bright with...humor? "FRIENDS."

Gertrude has friends? Rolph thought, though chided himself for being surprised. He assumed monsters in the dungeons only existed to roam endlessly and fight when an adventurer had the misfortune of getting in their way.

"Who are they?"

"LIZARDFOLK. THEIR SCENT IS FADING, WE MUST CATCH UP." She cocked her head, considering, then gave a nod. "QUICKLY, LITTLE DINOSAUR, YES."

"Can you tell how long ago they passed through here?"

Gertrude sniffed again. "THIS MORNING."

"Do you think Eliard could be dead?"

"I HOPE NOT. I *WAS* LOOKING FORWARD TO EATING HIM." Gertrude's tone was forlorn. "BETTER ALIVE."

Rolph ignored her culinary note and thought back over the textbook pages from school about the lizardfolk. He knew that they appeared from the thirtieth floor and down. He couldn't remember, either, if lizardfolk ate people, or simply killed them. He suppressed a shiver. "Will I be safe?" He wondered aloud.

Gertrude growled low. "WITH ME? YES. WITH MY COUSINS..." Whether the spell ran out again, or she simply left him in suspense, Rolph would never know.

Chapter Nine
Are They Going to Eat Me?

The next few hours passed with Gertrude in the lead and Rolph trailing behind, eyes darting back and forth scanning the broadening expanse of the cavern. He had never been one for caves, the dank and mold had made his nose run terribly and he didn't enjoy the insects and other creatures populating mundane caves.

The Labyrinth was no normal cavern system. It was wide enough in places where Rolph couldn't see any walls, or they were lost in darkness enough to make no difference. The ceilings were well above Gertrude's head, and it had the feel of an endless, moonless night above ground.

The purple blood of the lizardfolk faded and the dinosaur lost the trail, dismayed keening coming from her massive jaws. Rolph was about to cast his spell for the third time that day, though his reservoir of magic was dwindling the same as the day before, when he caught a glimpse of movement in the distance.

"Over there!" he called out and pointed, forgetting that Gertrude couldn't actually understand him. Luckily, she followed the direction of his finger and padded loudly forward. Rolph followed and an edge of the cavern came into focus. He couldn't tell what movement he had caught but as they approached the rock wall resolved into many small openings. Pockmarks the size of small people covered the stone face. The ambient glow of the caverns wasn't enough for Rolph to make out any details, so he took one of the torches from his pack and struck it alight.

Rolph stepped forward warily and as he passed in front of what appeared to be a particularly deep hole, eyes shone back at him for a moment before disappearing. He knew predators' eyes reflected light when hunting at night, and fear settled around his heart. Rolph waved to get Gertrude's attention and pointed at that particular tunnel. She stepped forward and stuck her nostrils into it with a thunk, breathing in deeply enough that a breeze drew at him coming from another carved opening.

They must be connected tunnels...

Gertrude brought her nose out and shook it, dust falling as she did so. Rolph jumped as she let out an ear-splitting roar. Then, she waited. Rolph wasn't sure what they were waiting *for*, but the Tyrannosaurus seemed to know what she was doing.

It wasn't long before a tiny reptilian snout poked out from the darkness of the tunnel Gertrude had snuffled in. As it came into the light of Rolph's torch, he made out the face of a young lizardfolk. He had no way to know whether it was male or female, nothing in his books gave him any indication of the difference. The creature stepped tentatively out of the rough entryway, gazing up at Gertrude with what Rolph could only describe as awe.

It yelled back into the cave in a guttural, raspy, language. Then, in the span of two heartbeats, it ran forward and threw itself to its knees at the dinosaur's feet, bowing forward and placing its hands on the ground. Echoes of the same tongue, which made Rolph's skin crawl, erupted from the various openings, followed shortly thereafter by more lizardfolk.

They came in various shapes and sizes, adults and children by the look of them, and prostrated themselves before Gertrude. Once they hit some kind of critical mass, a chant began, led by the small one who had started the strange ritual. Rolph's mouth hung open, and he stared at Gertrude who returned his look with a knowing reptilian grin.

Before he could stop himself, he cast his communication spell. "What, in the name of the Maiden, is going on?"

Some of the lizardfolk farther away from the feet of the dinosaur paused in their chanting to focus on Rolph. They hissed in unison, then returned to their bowing. *Did they just shush me?* He couldn't help but feel offended, somehow.

"THEY WORSHIP ME, SUPPERLING," she said, and instead of shushing her, the crowd below cheered ecstatically. Her voice, clear to Rolph though loud, had no translation for the worshippers. They must have heard it as a roar and made their own interpretation.

"How...did this happen?" Rolph wondered, a little more quietly than he had a sentence before. The lizardfolk at their feet shot him another withering glare but didn't shush him again, overcome with the chanting.

Gertrude gave him a dinosaur's equivalent of a shrug, given her tiny shoulders, and preened. The predatory ego made Rolph roll his eyes, but he couldn't help but crack a smile. Considering the difficult life (lives?) she'd led, he was grateful she had some respite, even if it was in the form of being worshipped.

Once the small lizardfolk in front was done chanting, it peeled itself from the floor and bowed deeply over its arms. It hissed a few words and Gertrude bowed her head, as though accepting a blessing. Then, the lizardfolk stood in unison and encircled them, all cheering and shouting in that same painful, hissing language. The press of the crowd pushed Rolph forward through the tunnel in the rock.

"Where are they taking us?" Rolph asked, but the spell had worn off. Gertrude blew a stream of hot air from her nostrils, and as they drew him deeper into the hole the smugness dancing in her eyes shrank away from his view. He planted his feet amid the press of bodies but a lizardfolk nearby made an annoyed noise and pushed him forward. Rolph hoped he was safe by association with Gertrude, if nothing else but for being the dinosaur-god's pet.

The tunnels led on for quite a way down. The loud whooping and hollering echoed around them. Rolph remembered the shaking in his home two days before (had it really only been two days?) and reconsidered his assumption that the vibration was Gertrude's doing. Was his house falling apart at that very moment?

Eventually, they broke into a larger cavern, and Rolph's feet slowed to a sudden stop. The view ahead of them left him completely breathless.

The tunnel opened into a kind of atrium. Three tiers of pathways crisscrossed in a downward spiral that must have run several stories deep. Strange looking mushrooms decorated the walkways, lit by the same strange glowing lights from the outside dungeon, and illuminated crystals. To Rolph's surprise, pockets along the boundaries of the walkways were filled with lamplight. *Are those homes?* he thought, his jaw sliding open. Some of the living spaces were chiseled into the stone, some of them utilized natural occlusions in the rocks.

He cast about, trying to find Gertrude and neared panic when she emerged from a much larger opening a hundred feet away from where he had entered. There must have been a bigger tunnel further on that he hadn't seen. A happy roar preceded her appearance and as she stepped onto the main thoroughfare more lizardfolk joined the parade. Some young, some old, as far as Rolph could tell, all of them excited to witness Gertrude in all her T-Rex glory.

They led them down two tiers and into a large pocket—or what Rolph could safely call buildings at this point—that could fit Gertrude. Long, wooden tables filled the brightly lit space, and the familiar scent of ale tickled Rolph's nose. Gertrude wriggled in on her belly, letting out a happy, dignified growl, as the lizardfolk barkeeper cracked open a large keg for her.

Meanwhile, lizardfolk closed in on them, each of them wanting to step a bit closer to Gertrude, which caused Rolph to stumble back several steps from her side. Immediately, his former space was filled with zealots, leaving him with no way to get back to her. Rolph reached for his communication spell, hoping to grab her attention, but the magic didn't surface. In any case, Gertrude was far too distracted sampling the dishes being offered to her large maw and accepting reverent touches.

A lizardfolk bumped Rolph's shoulder, tongue tsking as it passed. "You wish to ssspeak with usss? Trivial ssspell, human." The lizardfolk's voice was deep and raspy. "But we need no ssspellsss here."

"You can understand me?" Rolph asked, surprised. He hadn't known until this point how intelligent lizardfolk were, and his education had clearly been lacking.

The lizardfolk gave him a baffled look. "Of courrssse we can. We ssspeak the common tongue, even in these depthsss." It looked about them and snickered. "I've already paid my ressspectsss to the Great Mother. You are Her pet?"

Great Mother? The parallels with his own goddess gave Rolph pause. He gnawed on his lip, uncertain whether it would give him a leg up or harm him in the long run. "Something like that," he compromised.

"You mussst drink with me," the lizardfolk took his elbow and hauled him through the crowd. "The Mother will sssleep after she hasss eaten her fill."

Rolph cast a look over his shoulder at Gertrude. True to the lizardfolk's word, Gertrude was clearly enjoying herself. She wouldn't move for a time. He hesitated. They'd come to find

Eliard. "I have a question," he asked his handler, as he was pulled through the throng of folk. "We were tracking our prisoner, he's human like me. Do you know what happened to him?"

The lizardfolk raised its brow bones at him and gave a knowing smirk. "He will be okay, he isss, asss you sssay, alssso out cold. You are free to drink."

Well. That answered that question, then. If Gertrude felt safe here, and they accepted him as her companion, he must be protected. And if she thought he was in danger, she would have warned him, wouldn't she? Except she definitely seemed distracted enough. But they hadn't harmed him yet, and if they were going to slit his throat, they outnumbered him enough to do it in what passed as daylight.

Rolph grinned sheepishly and extended his hand. "I accept your offer. My name is Rolph."

"Excccellent! You may call me Mazden." The lizardfolk clasped wrists with him and led Rolph further into what clearly operated as a tavern.

Together they bellied up to a bar carved from the stone itself. While they waited to be served, Rolph examined their handiwork. Everything was rough-hewn, with no polish to be seen. Perhaps they had finer establishments or dwellings, but so far nothing he had seen showed a level of craftsmanship to rival even his own meager work.

His inspection was interrupted when a chunky wooden mug full of something as brown as the vessel it came in appeared before him, liquid sloshing over the side and splashing his hand.

"Mossst delverssss don't make it thisss far, human." Mazden lifted a mug of their own and held it out to toast.

Rolph hoisted his and clonked against Mazden's, then held the brew under his nose while Mazden eyed him. It had an earthy nose, almost like a soup, but a slight burn of alcohol tickled his nostrils.

I've come this far, he thought. *Poison would be a disappointing way to go.*

Rolph raised his mug again in salute and took a deep draw. It was certainly fermented, with a fragrant character and full body. It wasn't like the stouts or ales at home, but a distant cousin with a strange haircut. He couldn't place the flavor, and his brows furrowed in confusion as he set the mug down.

Mazden chuckled and seemed to take pity on Rolph. "*Bucha.* Mushroomsss. Most outsiders don't care for it, but it will grow on you."

"Like a fungus?" Rolph offered, as a spare joke.

Mazden stared at him for a solid thirty seconds, and Rolph began to worry he had somehow offended them. Eventually, however, a mighty hiss emanated from Mazden's mouth like a tea kettle overflowing. The only clue Rolph received was when the lizardfolk pounded their fist against the bar, then turned to their neighbor and said something in their raspy tongue.

The strange whistle traveled around the tavern as the joke made its translated way around the room, and Rolph finally joined in with Mazden. The lizardfolk wiped a tear from its eye and drank more of its mushroom beer. Rolph, feeling quite proud of himself for making a good impression on his hosts, tried to savor more of his strange beverage.

By the end of the third mug, he agreed the flavor had grown on him. That, or his taste buds had been obliterated by the alcohol, and it no longer mattered. In either case, Rolph was extremely comfortable with his place in the world for the first time in...well, ever. Perhaps things were looking up. He leaned over to his drinking companion, curious whether Mazden had heard of the guardian he was looking for.

"Ssso," he said, slurring his speech enough to sound like a native. "Have you heard of this 'pet master'?"

Mazden cocked their head to the side like Rolph had grown a second head. "The what?"

"Not what, who. The mini boss with the pet it summons from a necklace. Eliard, the man we're tracking, told us he could lead us to it."

"The bucha isss getting you too, I think."

"No, it's why we're here. Gertrude—uh, the Mother, wants to leave the Labyrinth and I need a way to bring her with me."

The silence which fell across the tavern was sudden and complete.

"Sssay that again," Mazden demanded.

"She...wants to leave the Labyrinth."

Mazden's tongue flicked in and out of their mouth angrily. "And how do you know thisss?"

"I spoke with her."

The anger in their eyes was replaced with a kind of respect. "You ssspeak the Mother's tongue?"

"Sometimes..."

"You are a Druid, then? Speaker of animal tongues. We never sssee your kind, though have heard tell of them."

Am I? He wondered what the one spell would constitute, from that perspective, but had been fighting for his life enough to not think about it until now. "I guess I am. Why don't you see Druids around here?"

"Our people have no such designations, we are sssimple folk. But you delversss, the onesss who make it this deep, are...different."

"How so?" Rolph sipped more bucha, the taste really had grown on him. The conversations around them picked up, and the hairs on the back of Rolph's neck finally lay down again.

"Those powerful enough to travel thisss far ssseek few things. Either more power, or an exit. Sssometimes it takesss one to get the other. Our people suffer for thisss." Mazden lapsed into silence without further explanation. Eventually they shook themselves out of whatever painful reverie they had conjured. "But who are we to question the will of the Mother?" Mazden drained the remainder of their cup, slamming it onto the bar with a crack. "Alasss, I know nothing of thisss 'pet massster' you ssspeak of."

Rolph's thumb traced the grain in his mug. It wasn't any surprise Eliard had misled them. It wouldn't be so far out of the realm of possibility that he would have lied to them to save his life. Or, a simpler explanation: Eliard didn't *actually* know anything, and had been hoping for his release. He squeezed the bridge of his nose, the last few days' events rolling over him in complicated and frustrating shapes and sounds in his mind's-eye.

"Do you know how I might be able to honor the Mother's wishes to leave?" he asked.

Mazden's lip curled in a smug grin. "That all dependsss, traveler," they took a deep drink from their mug and drummed their talons on the table. "What can you offer usss in exchange?"

Chapter Ten

IN THE LAND OF THE BLIND

What could Rolph offer? The question spun in his mind as he went to fetch Eliard the next morning.

The Shulzuh people, as Rolph had come to learn their name, had also allowed Rolph access to the holding cells where Eliard had been incarcerated. And Gertrude, as it happened, was greatly hungover and demanded rest. At least, that was the best Rolph could guess, given her grumbling and growling that next morning. The Shulzuh hadn't moved her, only draped her large body with flowers and lined her with painted stones. The priest had even thrown skins over her back like blankets, but none of them quite stretched all the way over her.

Mazden had found a boarding space for Rolph to sleep the night before, allowing that he followed through on his promise the following day. And thus, the stonemason slash druid slash bumbling adventurer found himself descending the carved steps of the makeshift prison behind a lizardfolk guard with a ring of keys. He was surprised that in the dankness of the cave, he had not experienced his usual sneezing or coughing fit. His best guess was that his new druid distinction had rid him of his pesky allergies.

"Thank you, Linath. At least I'll die here with a clear nose," he muttered beneath his breath, and was rewarded with a strange look from the guard.

Where Rolph had slept in a surprisingly comfortable bed made of moss covered in skins, Eliard had no such luxury. He was dirty, bloody, and slumped against the wall. "Couldn't fix your wounds?" he asked. "I thought you were a cleric."

Eliard's gaze shot up at the sound of Rolph's voice. His face turned a ghostly pale. "You?" the man managed. They must not have given him water, because his voice, like his lips, were cracked.

Rolph shrugged. "They're letting me take you, since you were our rightful prisoner to begin with." He planted his hands on his hips. "But I wonder what I should do with you."

Eliard scrambled to the wooden door, grasping the rungs. The wood must have been enchanted in some way to keep their inhabitants contained within. In any case, it was a pitiful sight to behold. "I'm sorry for running away," Eliard pleaded, "Please don't let them eat me."

Rolph exchanged a glance with the guard, who gave him a pointed *Like we would ever,* look of disgust at the mere mention. According to Mazden the night before, magic users weren't particularly tasty morsels. Neither were humans, as a general rule, unless there was a great shortage of food. No, they had found Eliard after he had escaped his bonds and intended to use him for a laborer, at best.

Rolph shrugged this thought away. Eliard didn't need to know. "That all depends on you, Eliard," he crouched down to the man's level. "I have it on good authority you not only escaped, which I can understand—but you also lied to me."

Eliard's bottom lip quivered and in that moment Rolph wondered whether Eliard was more of a coward than he was.

In all of Rolph's short acquaintance with the cleric, he had never known the man to do anything other than try to save his own skin. He remembered Rosalind snapping at Eliard to shut up, and guessed the behavior was not limited to being held captive to a strange druid and a dinosaur.

"I'll do anything. I swear, I didn't know. I *don't* know."

Rolph scratched at his jaw, and the stubble that had grown there over the past few days. "That's good to know. *Anything*, you say?"

Eliard nodded adamantly. "Yes! Yes! Please, just let me out!"

Rolph motioned to the guard, who unlocked the cell. "Great," he dragged the man onto his feet by his collar and set a bag of tools into his hands. "You'll carry these for me, then."

If he could draw Eliard's baffled expression, it would be a satisfying memory to keep forever. As though walking through a haze, Eliard dutifully followed Rolph up the stairs and out into the street followed by the guard, his arms laden with the equipment Rolph had given him to carry.

Rolph bent to ask the guard before they stepped onto the street. "About those bars, are they reinforced?"

The guard grinned. "Not in the ssslightessst," he told him in a low voice, as though sharing a delightful secret.

Rolph supposed the implicit threat of becoming a meal was enough to keep most people from attempting to escape. The keys in the guard's possession were rough creations, made of heavy cast iron. The lock had appeared to be just as primitive. Glancing at the weapon at the lizardfolk's hip, the cudgel with rough metal studs didn't strike him as particularly finessed. He had requested a makeshift set of tools, piecemeal from Mazden as they didn't possess a stonemason among them. *Then again...* he mused. *Maybe my offer is worth more than I thought.*

"Do you have a quarry here?" he asked.

The guard's expression was all the answer he needed, and he nodded to himself as they passed down the street and across a stone-hewn bridge spanning a small river. Normally he wouldn't have carried his tools on an exploratory trip, but with Eliard at his side, he decided it would build some character in the man.

When Mazden had asked what he could offer, Rolph had no idea. He was still riding a bit on the high of survival at the time and not an insignificant amount of buch to brighten his spirits. In the morning, he had stared at the lone mason's hammer next to the makeshift bed. The sight coalesced a number of his observations into a surprising conclusion. The lizardfolk were even worse at working stone than *he* was. Crafts, in general, were not their strong suit.

Rolph led Eliard past his theoretical job site. He had visually picked it on the way out of his lodgings that morning, borne on an inkling of a plan. No quarry meant no raw material to work, so his path took him out of the main tunnels back into the larger cavern to scout for the right stone. He would be starting from scratch, which was a daunting proposition.

Mazden's stories from the night before, of delvers picking the lizardfolk as an opportunity for mass slaughter, and thereby power, sickened him. Their kindness might have been due to his association with their "Mother", but they had been good to him, nonetheless.

He had sought out Mazden for the tools, and proposed a number of improvements he could make to their tunnels and settlement. Mazden ran to confer with the leadership of the town, acting as his representative since their drinking session earlier, and returned with agreement.

First things first, and requiring the least of his own skills, would be some sort of gate. Even considering Champions, who might have the strength to obliterate something as simple as a stone door, Rolph thought it was worth reinforcing what he could of their home.

Eliard trailed behind him, carrying a sack full of chisels, wedges, and hammers. The lizardfolks' metalworkers may have been rough, but they could still make a solid tool. They had also augmented his kit with several steel spikes and other bits scavenged from the rare delvers who made it this far and didn't survive to face the guardian.

Once outside the confines of the town, Rolph's anxiety blossomed again. Eliard started at every noise, which didn't help in the slightest. He would have to keep this trip short and come back with a guard of some kind if he found what he needed. Thankfully, being this far underground, he was spoiled for choice. Within a relatively short distance of one another, he found limestone, sandstone, granite, and quartzite. Back in his old life, a quarry like this would have been worth its weight in gold to his father. In this case, it was simply a means to an end.

To Eliard's obvious relief, they returned to the settlement. Gertrude had awakened in the meantime, and he found her drinking water from a carved trough, a pained expression on her face.

"Too much buch for you, too?" He chuckled, and Gertrude's miserable face needed no translation. The absurdity of his situation struck him then, commiserating with a T-Rex over her headache.

He shook his head and went to find Mazden. In short order, he had commissioned a small selection of guardspeople to accompany him. Soon, they travelled in a clatter of spears and hissed conversation to his planned quarry. Rolph hemmed and hawed over his choices and eventually settled on a black quartzite stone outcropping veined with white. He made his way ten feet up and set to his work.

As he raised his mason's hammer over the chisel to take the first swing, he flashed back to Reva Magnusdottir berating him over his window frames. It was the fiddly finish work that always tripped him up. The artistic vision of his father hadn't passed so easily to his son, and Rolph had always had an easier time with the rough shaping of the materials. He couldn't look at a block of stone and see the final florets his father would carve into a lintel or frame.

What he *could* do was see the veins and grains, where a stone would split, and how to shape it into the larger pieces his father excelled at refining. For the first time in his life, the part he was good at *mattered*. He brought the hammer down to begin making the first of many cuts and the tears in his eyes blurred his vision enough that the second took him in the thumb.

As he yelled his mixed frustration and joy, none of the onlookers could tell which it was. Which was fine, for Rolph. He knew, now, what he was going to do.

Chapter Eleven

WE'RE GONNA NEED A MONTAGE

It took three days in the quarry to get the slabs he wanted split just right.

Three days that consisted of far more trips than Rolph truly wanted to spend on the thing. The first day, he spent several hours working around his bruised thumb and a few missed aims of the chisel. His father once said the stone spoke to him, and Rolph was beginning to understand what he meant by that. Now that he had more confidence in himself, the work was going a lot more smoothly than it had back home. Rolph used Eliard to his full capacity. He was assigned his own personal guardsperson to get water from Shulzuh for them. He also had him draw and redraw lines along the stone as he worked more and more of the rockface away. He had him carry tools and bulky fragments away from the site.

The guardspeople got bored. They lounged at their posts and played games with dice carved from bone. Rolph didn't understand the rules much, when he paused in his work for a drink of water, only that when one of the lizardfolk rolled a seven, they all jumped and cheered. He made a mental note to try and learn it later.

It ended in a wrestling match between two of the guards, and Rolph's hammer arm was too sore to contemplate intervening. Plus, there was the matter of hauling his project back to Shulzuh, once he'd quarried what he wanted, that he had to resolve.

That took a bit of bucha and a talk with Mazden about pack-animals before bed. He checked in on Gertrude and found she'd retired early.

The second day, he came armed with a pack animal, a cleric, and another group of guards. Finally, he sectioned off the pieces of stone that resonated with him: thick with white marbling. Eliard and some of the guards used the beast of burden, which was more a four-legged lizard-not-dinosaur than anything he'd seen above-land, to haul four of the pieces away before lunch time. And then, on the fifth piece, he tweaked a muscle in his lower back and resorted to rest.

Gertrude had a field day with him that day, down at the bucha bar. She rolled on her stomach and guffawed when he limped in and cast his speaking spell. "WHAT IS THIS, SUPPERLING?"

Eliard was able to heal some of it once Gertrude stopped laughing.

Then, on the third day, with renewed vigor and an un-tweaked back, Rolph finished quarrying the last two slabs of quartzite.

He never did learn the rules of the dice game.

Eliard and his guards set the slabs where Rolph had designated the gate to be the previous day, and so it was easy to start putting them together. He worked with their blacksmith, who was named Kedreh, to make a rough set of hinges. They wouldn't be pretty but had to be strong. He intended to do his best to fit the gate in such a way that three lizardfolk at most would be needed to open or close it.

The problem was, he was no engineer despite being a mediocre mason and a halfway competent quarryman. In the end, he and

Kedreh assembled the gate, and a cheer went up from the crowd that had gathered to witness the final work. The good news was that the dark stone proved to be a stout barrier.

The bad news, which made the cheer die off as they realized it, was his installation proved too good at keeping the gate *closed*. Rolph only trapped them in the settlement for half a day, and when the gate finally swung smoothly—well, mostly smoothly—open, the smaller crowd which had remained let out a cry louder than the first.

Mazden approached, accompanied by the leaders of the village, who nodded appraisingly at what Rolph had done. Mazden slapped Rolph on the back and hissed a reptilian grin. "You did it, human."

"Indeed," Rolph agreed, trying to stuff down his own pride at the accomplishment. No one had ever cheered for him before, and his chest swelled from the accolades of the town. "Crone take you, Reva."

"What wasss that?"

Rolph cleared his throat, embarrassed. "Nothing."

"Well, it isss a good ssstart." Mazden clapped him on the shoulder and began to walk back toward the center of town.

"Wait a minute. What do you mean, a start?"

Mazden turned and smiled, his tongue flicking in and out. "That wasss the first gate, yesss? We have more tunnelsss for you to ssseal."

"Now hold on, I never agreed—"

"Unlesss you don't want to know how to sssave the Mother."

Rolph considered the nebulous "deal" he had made and whether he had negotiated poorly, by which he realized he hadn't negotiated at all. He grumbled to himself, turning back to the gate. *It does look good*, he thought to himself, then quailed as he mentally counted the openings he had seen when they arrived.

The reward for a job well done was always more work, even ninety-five levels below the surface.

Some things never change.

The pattern repeated itself for a time. Every three days or so, Rolph would complete a gate. The town would cheer, though the group which gathered each time grew smaller and smaller. Eventually one of the lizardfolk who had been a regular attendant shadowed Rolph during his working days. After a week Rolph handed her, as she turned out to be a female named Kerzat, a hammer and chisel and showed her how to read the layers in the stone.

Throughout the day, Rolph chuckled to himself as she smashed her thumbs more than once, then chided his own behavior as too reminiscent of task-masters he'd had in the past. Kerzat learned quickly, however, and soon was acting as a sort of apprentice to Rolph. She would mark the stones, he would begin the jobs, and then she would pick up where he designated the proper cuts to be.

One day while taking a break punctuated by the rhythm of Kerzat's hammer strikes, he encountered a small object in his pouch while fishing for a bit of dried mushroom to eat. Eliard had been conjuring food for the two of them to supplement what the residents of Shulzuh ate, but Rolph had grown fond of some of their staples.

He drew the thing out and found the ring he had taken from Ross's body. Loot wasn't anything he ever expected to receive, given the admonition at his birth, but he turned the simple gold band over in his fingers. Normally finding something like that in the Labyrinth meant having it assessed for curses or negative effects.

It was unlikely that Ross, Champion that he was, had decided to wear a cursed ring.

"Why not?" he asked aloud. Kerzat paused and glanced over at him, but he waved her back to her work.

The ring was oversized for him, but as Rolph placed it over the tip of his index finger the circle shrank until it was a perfect fit. He had never worn a magic ring before and didn't know what to expect. Would it tingle? Burn? Would the darkness open before him as if it were lit with a hundred torches? He slipped it on without effort and waited.

Nothing happened, which was an average experience for Rolph. He shrugged and signaled to Kerzat. "Break's over!"

The lizard woman's breathing was rapid and shallow, and her tongue flicked quickly in and out. She nodded gratefully at Rolph and passed him the tools. He lined the chisel up on her last striking point, raised the hammer, and brought it down in a skillful stroke.

The stone, which had been nowhere near ready to calve, split with a loud crack. Despite being iron, the chisel's end mushroomed from the blow. If his hammer hadn't been good Mayfair steel, it likely would have deformed the same.

"Linath's grace!" he exclaimed, looking between his hands and the stone.

Lizardfolk didn't whistle, but Kerzat made a kind of astonished buzzing sound that Rolph had learned to interpret the same way. The two stared at each other for a minute before Rolph broke the silence with a gleeful laugh.

Things were going to go *much* faster now.

Chapter Twelve
IS SOMEONE CUTTING ONIONS?

Rolph's enhanced strength made quicker work of his task list than before. The dirty looks Kedreh gave him for ruining perfectly good chisels led to an improvement in the quality of Shulzuh ironwork by necessity.

In addition to all of the gates, the leaders of the settlement had convinced Rolph to complete a few more projects. They accomplished this mostly by silently adding items to his list when he wasn't paying attention, and then looking innocently at him when he reprimanded them for it. Eventually he kept the list tucked into his shirt near his heart to prevent his "Rolph do" list from getting any longer.

It was a month later when Rolph placed the final hinge for the last gate.

This time, there were only three lizardfolk to cheer for him upon this completion. He nodded politely to them and excused himself as quickly as he was able. He'd agreed to some bucha with Kerzat and Mazden in quiet celebration, but he was exhausted.

As much as he wanted to hear what the secret was that Mazden had kept from him in exchange for his labor, Rolph needed to rest. It probably wouldn't matter much if he didn't show up.

He parted with Kerzat with half-promises of *maybe* appearing at the crossroads between the tavern and where he was staying. Since he'd been so busy with the Shulzuh leader's list of to-dos, he'd only seen Gertrude a handful of times in the past week. She always seemed to light up when he came into view, which was comfort enough that she hadn't forgotten him, or had gotten bored waiting on their departure. Still, it had been surprisingly quiet without the dinosaur following him.

He had sent Eliard off on a sort of fool's errand to get him out of the way earlier and wasn't expecting him back anytime soon.

It was the perfect opportunity for rest.

Or at least he thought.

Mazden caught him outside the inn he was staying at. They leaned against the stone wall with their arms crossed, as though they'd been waiting for Rolph to ditch out on their planned "party."

Rolph couldn't contain his disappointed groan. "I really can't take on anymore work, Maz."

"Yesss, you've done well," Mazden told him. "I thought you might need sssome ressst. Come, let's chat."

They led Rolph into the inn and up to a quiet seating area looking out over the rest of the building. "Are you finally going to tell me what I can do for the, uh…Mother?" In the month that Rolph had stayed among the Shulzuh, he had never gotten used to Gertrude's title.

"You *have* earned it," Mazden affirmed. "With great honorsss," they added, taking a seat on one of a set of chairs. Rolph took the other.

"How long are you going to hold me in suspense for? I was looking forward to a nap."

Mazden made a clicking sound halfway between a chuckle and a tsk, which Rolph had come to learn was a sound of amusement.

"Lisssten closssely, then. Thisss whole level is a labyrinth. There isss another gate you may be able to use, one large enough for the Mother to transversssse. It isss in the heart of another maze at the center of the Labyrinth."

Rolph squinted at the lizardfolk who, in many ways, had become a friend. At least a general buddy. A fond acquaintance. "Where are we relative to the center of the Labyrinth?" he asked.

Mazden pulled out a thin slab of rock, on which had been carved winding and crossing lines. Rolph couldn't make heads or tails of the markings until Mazden tapped a talon on one of the squiggles along the edge. "Shulzuh is here." They moved their finger to the center of the stone "map." "And here is the sssecond gate."

Rolph didn't want to tell them the map appeared...well, frankly *useless,* in its current state. "And you're certain that Gert–The Mother will be able to fit through?"

"Certain? No. A better chance, though."

Rolph drummed his fingers on his leg, thinking. "How far away would you say this gate is?"

Mazden shrugged. "Ssseveral daysss at leassst."

Rolph winced. He had already paid his dungeon insurance for the month, but he would need to get home sooner than later or risk losing his parents' shop. They would need to get moving, and soon.

So much for that nap.

"Right," Rolph stood. "I better go build up our supplies then."

Mazden stood with him and passed him the map. "Keep it, human. Visssit any time."

Rolph spent the rest of the evening gathering supplies for himself, Gertrude, and, regrettably, Eliard. The Shulzuh had released Eliard into Rolph's custody, and in his custody the cleric would stay. They didn't have any reason to keep him around, and Eliard still flinched when they came too close.

By the time he finished purchasing rations with the meager funds he'd gathered in his employ (tips, really), Eliard finally caught up to him. "Rolph!" he called to the stonemason as he came up the street.

Rolph's patience deteriorated ever further. "Eliard," he greeted the cleric.

"I wasn't able to find the knox weed you asked for, or any dotted rope," Eliard told him apologetically. Rolph fought the temptation to smirk. Of course he hadn't, the things never existed, he just needed a break. Since he'd "saved" Eliard from his holding cell, the man had been insufferably *present*. At his elbow at all times, asking what he could do for Rolph. "But I did find you some of those partridge eggshells. Are you using them to make paint?"

Rolph accepted the offered pouch in grim surprise. "Something of the sort. Hey, you did great today." He slapped the man on the shoulder. "I'm sure you need some rest. Can you do me a favor if you're heading down to the tavern?"

"Sure! Of course, anything!"

Rolph grimaced. He'd figure out some way to get the man to stop groveling around him. "Can you tell Gertrude to meet us at the gate first thing in the morning? We're heading out. You be ready, too?" The thought of Eliard trying to communicate fine details to Gertrude put a smile on Rolph's face. It would keep the other man busy, for a while anyway. Rolph had already told Gertrude when they were leaving.

"Sure thing," Eliard saluted. "Am I good to go?"

"Yes. Go enjoy your evening, I'm going to get some rest."

"You've got it, boss!"

Eliard turned heel and left before he could see Rolph wince.

This was going to be a very, *very* long trip.

Rolph found Gertrude the next morning stretching her back near the front gate. Her large head swiveled, and her bright eyes sparkled. The purring in her carnivorous chest sounded almost feline to the trained ear—and potentially frightening to one who might not have heard it before.

He saved his magic for now but patted her on the snout when she bent down. It amazed him how comfortable he had gotten with the enormous beast in what was a relatively short amount of time, all things considered. They had begun to understand each other, at least partially, even without the spell. Which was a good thing, given how infrequently he was able to use it.

Rolph shouldered his pack, weighed down by enough mushroom jerky to choke a lizard-horse as well as whatever other sundries he'd managed to bargain for from the shopkeepers. Luckily for him, he seemed to be in the whole town's good graces and knew he had gotten a better deal than any human had a right to in this subterranean town.

He motioned for Gertrude to head toward the largest of the tunnels, so they could make their exit, but she didn't budge. She only cocked her head to the side in a questioning way.

"Well," he said, "You understand me some of the time, anyway."

Gertrude heaved a great sigh, as if she might have been thinking the same thing. Eliard took that moment to burst into view, his own pack on his shoulders, bedroll half-secured and bouncing wildly with his strides.

"Not leaving without me, are you?" He grinned at the two of them. Gertrude smiled back, but with the size of her teeth, it felt distinctly more predatory. Eliard's grin turned to a grimace, and he faced Rolph. "Ready to go?"

Rolph pondered briefly whether he would have wanted to leave Eliard behind. He had contemplated it, surely, but the reality of the Labyrinth was he was *far* out of his element. Having fallen in as far as he did, Eliard at least had been part of a successful delving party. No, he wouldn't leave the man behind if he could serve a purpose, that being helping them get out of this place alive.

"Let's go," Rolph said.

When they reached the end of the tunnel, the guard opened the way and gave them a hasty salute before swinging Rolph's stone creation shut behind them. As the gate closed, Rolph felt a pang of something bittersweet. He placed his hand on the roughhewn surface. He had made this, with no one to lead or chide him.

They began walking along the path, Mazden's map fresh in his mind to guide their steps. He stared at his palm as they went, the gold band encircling his finger a stark counterpoint to his life before entering the maze.

It will have to be enough, won't it?

Chapter Thirteen

Are We There Yet?

"How far until we reach the central maze?" Eliard asked.

"Maiden's braids, Eliard. I have no idea," Rolph said, but quailed inwardly. In addition to not having any masons, Shulzuh clearly also didn't contain any cartographers. After their first full day of walking, they hadn't found any of the landmarks their map indicated would mark their progress to the middle of the Labyrinth.

"I told you," Eliard panted. "This level is huge. It took us weeks to cross it, and we never even encountered the true maze."

"Nobody likes to hear 'I told you so'. What were you doing here if you weren't trying to find the center, anyway?"

"We were done." Eliard wiped the sweat from his brow in counterpoint. "The wayfinder found the shortest path to the nearest gate home. We had enough of this. Half of the party didn't even want to come this deep, but we needed a majority vote to exit at the last portal."

Rolph had gotten an earful about Eliard's former "friends" as they traveled. They had formed a treasure hunting delving party, each member having an equal stake in the preparation and therefore cut of the spoils. Except most of them were greedy bastards.

When they entered the Labyrinth together, the goddesses held them to their agreement upon arrival. They could opt to exit at each gate to the next level, but that was only if the majority stake wanted to leave. So down they went, and further still, until they had traversed more of the Labyrinth than any of them had known before.

Rolph wheezed. The hard labor he had done, even aided by his erstwhile apprentice, had broadened his shoulders and strengthened his arms. It had not, however, done anything for his walking endurance. He was about to call a halt for rest when a particular outcrop of rock caught his eye. He held up a hand in a gesture he thought was appropriate to say "halt" but both Eliard and Gertrude kept walking, leaving him behind.

Rolph sighed and rolled his eyes, then stuck dust-covered fingers into his mouth and blew a loud whistle. The two of them swung their heads around in nearly identical gestures, despite the size difference.

"I think..." Rolph leaned over and rested his hands on his knees to catch his breath. "This is the first marker. That stone shaped like a lizardfolk's head?" He gestured vaguely in the direction of the oddly shaped rock formation.

Eliard walked closer to examine it, cocking his head to one side then the other. "I don't see it."

Rolph unshouldered his pack and fished the map out from its confines, holding it up for Eliard to see. "Look, it's right there. The nose, the tongue?"

"Maybe, it's just—"

The faint sound of something skittering nearby ground their conversation to a halt.

"What was that?" Eliard's voice cracked with fear.

Rolph rolled his eyes again, then cast his gaze about searching for something. The light was dim, as they had passed once again into adjoining cave systems lit by fungus. At the edges of his vision, he caught a glimpse of a large insect of some kind crawling into a fist-sized hole in the ground.

"It's just a bug, you coward," Rolph scoffed.

"*Just* a bug? I told you about the pet master and its cave crawler minion, didn't I?"

"And Mazden called you a liar. They'd never heard of either before. Well, they'd heard of cave crawlers but nothing about something keeping one as a *pet*."

"It was in a journal we found on a dead delver partway through the level," he pouted. "Least I think it was. I never saw it, but Skarn told me about it."

Rolph recalled being carried across the dwarf's sweaty back and shivered in disgust. "Yes, good old reliable Skarn. He was pulling your leg, Eliard."

The weakest monsters anyone had mentioned encountering were the minotaurs Rolph had found after his first steps onto the level. Finally seeing something relatively harmless was refreshing, though he reminded himself he didn't actually know much about cave crawlers beyond what Eliard had told him.

"They give me the creeps." Eliard gave an exaggerated shiver.

Rolph wandered over to where he had seen the critter scuttle and poked at the hole with his boot. He turned and rested his hands on his hips. "See? Nothing to worry about."

But Eliard had stopped looking at him and his gaze was fixed on something above Rolph's head. He opened his mouth to shout but not before something dropped heavily onto Rolph's shoulders. He fell to the floor and bright lines of pain exploded across his back. Gertrude's roar thundered around them and the pressure of whatever had knocked him over eased.

Rolph scrambled to his feet and turned, drawing his hammer from his belt and casting his one spell. "What was that?" He swept his gaze ahead of him and the wan light cast shadows across a horrifying creature.

If its six legs covered in sharp barbs weren't enough, its thick carapace made the tool in Rolph's hand look like a toothpick. The cave crawler, for that was surely what this monstrosity was, stood as tall as a pony, and twice as wide. No eyes graced its head, but long antennae swayed back and forth, probing the air around it.

Eliard, coward though he was, had set his lance with its broad spearhead pointed at the thing. It might have been black, or a deep reddish brown, but its chittering mandibles parted wide, and it hissed an insectoid scream in their direction. Gertrude stood on the other side of it, effectively flanking the monster.

"Gertrude, stomp!" Rolph cried.

Gertrude, eyes clear with understanding from the spell, raised one massive taloned foot and brought it crashing down on the giant bug. Its antennae quivered and before the pad of the dinosaur's foot came within a hand's width of crushing it, the crawler leapt to the side. Dust and dirt from the path rose into the air and covered them all from the power of her step.

"It's fast!" Eliard yelled, reorienting his point to keep it between him and the monster.

"You think?" Rolph said, voice dripping with sarcasm.

The cave crawler spun faster than Rolph would have expected and lunged for him. Rolph was no fighter, and had spent the last month quarrying stone, not training for battle. That said, between the hard labor and his new ring, his hammer arm was stronger than it had ever been.

Rolph did something no trained warrior would have done and ducked below the level of the monster's face. It left him vulnerable to attack from above, but he hoped his next move would negate the risk as he slammed his hammer down on the leading leg of the crawler. It had six, so perhaps damaging one might not do enough, but Rolph targeted the "knee" where it appeared to be jointed.

His unexpected attack caught the fleet-footed monster off guard enough that he struck home. Ichor sprayed where the thick shell cracked, and another inhuman scream came from the creature. It retreated perpendicular to the delvers and their dinosaur, turned, and crouched. Its back was to a wall now, but it was the only direction it could have gone. Rolph hadn't gotten a good look at whether his strike had hampered its movement, but he was simply glad to have hit it.

"Box it into the wall!" Rolph cried.

"AS YOU WISH, SUPPERLING," Gertrude said, and the massive insect's antennae trembled at the sound of her voice.

Rolph gestured for Eliard to move to his left, with Rolph in the center and Gertrude blocking the right. Like a three-tined fork, they approached the crawler. Gertrude leaned in to snap at its head, and it struck her nose viciously. She reared back with a cry but brought her razor sharp teeth back down to harry it as it tried to scuttle through her legs. Gertrude kicked at it and while she didn't squash it, she managed to shove it backward.

Eliard brought his spear to bear, stabbing at its less armored side, black blood seeping from the wound he caused. The spearhead lodged there, and Eliard set the shaft against his foot, trying to push it against the wall. Rolph took that moment to dart forward again, aiming for the other lead leg with his gore-flecked hammer face. With a crack, the crawler pitched forward, unable to balance itself.

As Rolph jumped back out of range, the crawler caught his arm in its mandibles and cut a deep gash above his left hand. The monster didn't let go, however, and gnawed at Rolph like a dog's chew toy. He screamed but kept enough of his wits about him to strike the creature between its antennae.

Once, twice, thrice, he continued hammering at its head until the grip of its mandibles slackened. Rolph freed his wrist, though his hand hung limply at the end of it. He gave one last swing of the hammer, spraying himself again liberally with ichor, before collapsing heavily to the ground.

The same warmth he had felt after the minotaur plummeted to its death over that cliff came once again. It suffused his body and lifted his spirits, though it was short lived. As the power coursed through his body and dissipated, he still had a useless hand and was losing more blood than he thought he could spare.

He lifted his arm and waved painfully at Eliard. "I think I..." he began to say, but consciousness fled, and he knew no more for a time.

Chapter Fourteen
DELVING IS FOR THE BIRDS

Rolph awoke propped against the wall, some feet away from the carcass of the slain monster. It took a moment for his awareness to settle into his body as the final fingertips of sleep slipped away from his mind. A small fire crackled nearby and something long and warm pressed against his leg. Exhaustion and pain riddled his body, and he let out a groan. He flexed his fingers experimentally and found his hand was no longer useless.

"Good morning, sunshine!" Eliard's voice called, and Rolph squeezed his eyelids shut.

Whatever it was that happened to him was more miserable than the worst hangover he'd ever experienced.

The large appendage pressed more firmly against him, and a low, reptilian growl rumbled through the stone he laid on. He slipped his arm around the end of her tail, realizing what it was. "I'm alright," he told her grimly, then peered back out from his heavy eyes. "What happened?"

"You're extremely lucky," Eliard had at some point walked over and was now standing in front of him, arms crossed and looking supremely proud of himself. "If you hadn't leveled at that moment, you'd have been a goner. I healed you the rest of the way while you were unconscious and drooling."

Rolph rubbed his forehead with his free hand, absentmindedly patting Gertrude's tail in the meantime. "What do you mean, leveled?"

"You are kind of hopeless, aren't you?" Eliard said in a pitying voice that made Rolph cringe.

"Explain," he grumbled, his patience, if it existed, wearing thin.

"Right, so!" Eliard clapped his hands together and crouched. "When a mommy delver and a daddy delver—"

"Be serious, Eliard. I feel too awful for jokes right now."

Eliard frowned but conceded. "When a delver enters the labyrinth for the first time, they are assigned a class. This is generally bestowed upon them by one of the goddesses. They enter as an Explorer. Once they start killing monsters, or gather resources, they absorb the essence of those things. That enhances you and eventually evolves your skills and power. Delvers have short-handed it to 'levels' since forever. You're of the distinction 'Adventurer' now, from what I can gather."

Rolph's mind decided it didn't want to retain any of what Eliard was saying halfway through his explanation, preferring to spin. "Right. Okay." He muttered as the world tilted away.

"When you level, you gain a little burst of health. If you're a magic user, you gain spells and power, and if you're a fighting class, you increase your stamina." He gestured at Rolph. "You also have class abilities bestowed on you by the Triad, though I'm not entirely certain of your class at this point. Given your propensity to talk to giant lizards—No offense," he said hastily at Gertrude. She gave Rolph an inquisitive look and Rolph shook his head. "I would say you're a magic user of some kind. Do you know what else you can do?"

Rolph squinted. "What else I can do?" He thought of the green magic that burst through his mouth when he cast the spell to speak with Gertrude. "What do you mean? Mazden called me a Druid, but I hadn't thought much about it at the time."

"Well, that's a lot better than me guessing about it. You could have told me sooner," Eliard complained.

"I was a bit busy, not much call for any of that when I'm working stone for a month."

Eliard nodded, considering. "Fair enough. Are there times where you feel like you can do...something and it happens?"

"Not that I'm aware of?" All of his life, Rolph had been on the exact opposite side of that spectrum: believing he could do something and realizing he was incapable of the task. "Can I think on it later?"

"Better, we can work on it later," Eliard slapped him on the shoulder. "In any case, time to get up and get some dinner. You'll feel better."

Rolph sincerely doubted it, with the quaking in his head, but he staggered to his feet anyways.

It bothered him that he was severely lacking in his understanding of the Labyrinth and the adventurers who delved within.

What made matters even worse, Eliard was right. Dinner did make him feel better.

Eliard began pushing Rolph to "discover his magic" the next morning. He insisted Rolph start small, but the stonemason argued against his method entirely.

"Can you move that rock?" He had asked at one point as they walked. Rolph had given him an incredulous look and walked over to it. "No, no! I mean, with your mind—no, your *magic!*"

"What does that have to do with being a Druid? Maybe I should try *talking* to it instead," Rolph said dryly.

"I don't know, I've never met one. It's worth trying everything," he insisted.

Eliard gave him a dirty look until he relented, raised a hand and stared at the stone until he was cross-eyed. Nothing happened, and he rolled his eyes at Eliard before setting off again.

Certainly, he had met mages. His mother was one, after all. He had heard time and time again that the quality of magic was like that of an essence you pulled from your heart of hearts. An extension of yourself, manifested into physical use. His parents had tested him at a young age for magic and had been told he had none. Now, thirty-some-odd years and an interesting tumble later, he was told he could harness it?

After a reasonably long day of traveling and a few monster encounters, they hadn't found any sufficient evidence that Rolph was magical at all beyond his ability to communicate with Gertrude.

Around the time they decided it was time to give up the search for the day and find a safe place to camp, a tickle of discomfort radiated up Rolph's spine. "Stop," he told them, and threaded some magic into his voice so Gertrude understood him as well. It was only the second time that day he had used it: the time before had been to reason her away from chasing a furry monster down a tunnel far too small for her.

Both of his companions stopped and turned. "What is it?" Eliard asked.

Rolph concentrated on the ground ahead of him and tilted his head this way and that. His vision shifted as if there was an exact angle at which whatever rankled the back of his brain would reveal itself. He squinted and mentally *pushed* against something, the tingle of magic leaving his body spread over him and a verdant glow appeared as a dot in the dirt, ten feet ahead of him.

The spot of green blossomed ahead of them, like a mist settling into the rocks. He cautiously stepped toward it, prodded around the edges of the large circle and found some of the ground gave way beneath his gentle prodding.

"It's a pitfall trap," Eliard explained with a low whistle behind him. He crouched beside Rolph and pressed his hand into another part of it. The dirt crumbled to reveal a silver, sticky web.

Rolph suppressed a shiver. "It's this whole circle," he pointed out the edges of the green radius.

"You see it?" Eliard asked, impressed.

"Yeah? You don't?" Rolph asked, mildly annoyed.

"No, I don't." Eliard grinned. "You can detect traps, then. You *are* a magic user."

The goddesses must have granted him another spell, for which Rolph was grateful. Being able to communicate with Gertrude had saved his life, but only having one trick wouldn't see him through the rest of the Labyrinth. Rolph rolled back onto his heels. "Be that as it may, it begs the question: what monster did this?"

Eliard's eyes darted to his, widening. "I don't want to meet the creature big enough to make *that*."

Rolph winced inwardly, the cleric had been too excited to recognize their predicament.

The pitfall left little room for them to continue on their path. The humans might have been able to by pressing themselves tightly against the wall–but Gertrude didn't have the luxury of a small body. Whatever arachnid monster had built this had made it large enough to be a threat even to the T-Rex. And chances were it would return soon to check its trap. The matter was whether it was behind or ahead of them, and if it was safer to turn around and risk running into the monster.

"Where do we go from here?" he asked the more experienced, if timid, delver. Eliard shrugged in mute reply. Rolph heaved a sigh and turned to the dinosaur again. "Gertrude, can you...uh...jump over this?"

Gertrude toed the circle with a giant foot, lifting it back out with the sticky tendrils of web clinging to her scales. She shook it out, smacking it against the ground in a gesture that reminded Rolph of a rabbit thumping its foot in irritation. "I CANNOT CROSS THIS GAP, SUPPERLING."

Eliard closed his hands over his chin and considered. "What could have made this?" He wondered, repeating Rolph's question to himself. "I don't recall seeing spiders this size, in the deep, but I guess it would make sense."

A shiver coursed down Rolph's spine, this time having nothing to do with magic. "Gertrude can't get across. Even if my power's enhanced, I can only talk to her, or find more traps like this, so many times." Rolph pulled Mazden's map from his pack and consulted it, but the detail wasn't fine enough to give him any clear options. "We'll have to find another way around."

Rolph would have given his weight in gold for a sturdy walking stick and he was praying silently to the Mother for a deep tree-root to scavenge when a length of wood caught his eye, strapped to Eliard's pack. They had kept everything they looted from the corpses of Eliard's companions, Fern's staff included. He was no wizard, but the staff would make for a convenient tool for testing the ground ahead of them as they walked.

Leading them back down the passage they had come through, Rolph took a reasonable looking fork which moved them back in the correct direction. The tap-tap of his walking stick echoed strangely in the depths. He hoped it wouldn't announce their presence, but it was better than falling face first into another pit.

Rolph's thumb traced the runes carved into the shaft as he walked. "Maybe you'll help me get out of here after all, Fern."

Chapter Fifteen
SECRETS UNKNOWN

The "several days" Mazden had predicted for their trip to the central maze of the Labyrinth had turned into more than a week. Eliard's conjured food grew tasteless and their days were a constant cycle of slow progress, checking for pits and other traps at all reasonable intervals. Eliard's fear had grown after they discovered the third trap in less than half a day after their initial finding. This led to a paranoia which only deepened over time.

"We should check again," he would say. Forget that Rolph wanted to save at least a thread of his miniscule pool of power to speak with Gertrude in an emergency. He reckoned it slowed their travel to a crawl and would delay them for weeks if he let Eliard have his way.

"Unless you've suddenly sprouted the ability to check yourself, Fern's staff is going to have to do, for the most part."

And on they went, Rolph tapping ahead and to the sides like a blind beggar in an alley. He only used his new spell when he felt it was worth the risk, like when they found themselves in a relatively narrow passageway between rock faces. It paid off, however, and that was when they found the first of the acid traps.

He triggered the trap with the staff and managed to only lose a strap on his pack when the angry liquid splashed onto it. The complexity of the traps had increased over time, and eventually they were avoiding falling rocks, along with the original pitfall style traps. The pair lost two days of travel to recover from their first encounter with a poison gas trap, with repeated healing from Eliard hastening the process. Rolph's lungs still itched when he thought about it.

Rolph wiped his brow as they crested a slight rise in the path. Ahead of them rose a large stone arch marking the entrance to the maze. "Crone's beard, it's about time."

His relief turned to apprehension as they continued forward. The distance was deceptive and by the time they reached the finely crafted arch, it towered above even Gertrude's head. The design departed significantly from the rest of the Labyrinth they'd traversed thus far. Where they had tread was cavernous and rough, like a naturally formed set of caverns even though they went on for miles. These enormous stones had been dressed and fitted by a master, or a god. Eliard gave a low whistle.

Rolph touched the smooth stone with his calloused palm. "Why do you think it's so big?"

Eliard gestured to Gertrude, who stood in the middle of the arch which framed her like a human standing in a normal doorway. "Makes me worry about what the Triad's placed in there, if the ceilings need to be so high."

The map in Rolph's hand ended where they stood, the gate drawn as a simple pictogram. He tucked it into his pack in case they needed it for a return trip. He had no reason not to trust the folks of Shulzuh, but that didn't mean they would be successful in their venture against the guardian here. Should they need to retreat, he wanted some kind of visual to guide them back to a safe area to recuperate a second time.

Torches lined the walls of the entry corridor of the maze, seemingly unaffected by fuel consumption as they each appeared to be brand new to Rolph's eyes. Despite the effort to conserve his magic, he chanced a detection spell before stepping foot into the maze proper. The green glow suffused the area and then dissipated, which meant there was nothing to worry about. Or at least nothing the spell could detect, but it hadn't failed him yet.

"Let's go," he said and strode into the long corridor.

They went about two hundred paces before a sharp fork in the hallway revealed itself. Nothing stood at the end waiting for them, despite Rolph's imagination assuming there would be some kind of armored warrior blocking their path. *Too many bedtime stories,* he grumbled to himself as they approached the decision point. Rolph examined their choices, and the right-hand corridor looked much like the left, with nothing differentiating the two besides the direction. He tapped at the floor of each with Fern's staff but that yielded no insight.

With a shrug, Rolph turned to the left and raised a boot to take the first step when Eliard's hand came to rest on his shoulder. The light touch froze him in place with his foot midair.

"Remember," Eliard said. "This is going to be different from what we've faced so far."

Rolph let his foot down when he realized he stood like a statue, waiting for something terrible to happen. He cleared his throat and turned to the man. "Different than slogging through unending traps and caverns?"

"Very."

Rolph stared at Eliard, waiting for more of an explanation.

Eliard let his breath out in a huff. "Don't you remember anything I tell you? This is where the treasure of the level is stored and protected. It's not only wandering monsters anymore."

"Yes, yes, the Guardian—"

"Not only that," Eliard cut in. "There will be monsters placed specifically to *guard* the approach to the Guardian, more traps, you name it."

"Is that going to influence which direction I choose..." Rolph asked but trailed off as a blur of motion behind Eliard caught his eye. He peered around the cleric to search for what it had been, but the way was clear.

Eliard moved to intercept Rolph's gaze. "What is it?"

"Something fast moved through that passage." He motioned to indicate the right-hand corridor, which had been behind Eliard during his last admonition.

Eliard whipped around and looked for himself but appeared to come up as empty-handed as Rolph had. "I guess we should go the other way, then? We leave whatever it was to our backs, but it might be worth the risk if we avoid it."

Rolph looked at Gertrude, who stared off into the distance, not paying attention to either of them. No help was going to come from her, but Rolph also didn't want to use the last of his magic for the day just to get her opinion. He nodded and turned once again to the passageway to the left.

His hopes for a smooth trip were dashed as soon as they had gone another few hundred paces. They came upon another fork, this time continuing straight and to the right. Rolph's mind spun trying to orient their direction compared to how they had entered the central Labyrinth, and he knew they would be lost in an instant.

"Eliard, you've done these central mazes before, right?"

The other man stood with his hands on his hips examining the new path. "Sure, why?"

"How did you keep from being turned around? My head is already spinning trying to decide which direction leads farther inward."

"Oh, we had Skarn," Eliard said in an offhand manner.

"Skarn again," Rolph spat under his breath.

"What was that?"

"Nothing." Rolph cleared his throat and checked his tone. Giving Eliard a hard time for relying on the party's pathfinder was like blaming water for being wet. "Assume we don't *have* a pathfinder. What do delving parties without one do?"

"Oh!" Eliard took his pack off and fished around until he came away with a large piece of chalk. "We still marked the way, in case Skarn was having an off day and we needed to backtrack. Without a pathfinder, it's one of the easiest ways to know where you've been." Eliard demonstrated by marking the wall to their left before the fork. "Left hand says it's the path you took to enter. So, you keep it on your right to get out."

The practice agreed with the practical part of Rolph's brain. "Right or straight, then?"

"If I'm thinking about this correctly, turning here heads into the maze."

Rolph had no reason to object, so he turned and made his way in that direction. Eliard marked the stone on their left as they went. The first few turns took minutes of deliberation but eventually they gave up on agonizing over each choice and quickly chose the path they deemed most likely to lead deeper into the maze.

Rolph couldn't decide if they were actually making progress but counted forward momentum as something. His successful encounter with the cave crawler, despite nearly losing his hand over it, had boosted his confidence in his ability to handle dangerous situations. He mused on whether that was either earned or wise but had no answer to the question.

More than one dead-end caused them to retrace their steps, adding to the overall confusion but proving Eliard's chalking method. The cleric had earned some new respect in Rolph's eyes, and Rolph was forced to remember that despite being a coward, he had survived ninety-four levels of the Labyrinth before their party finally decided to call it quits. Rolph trusted Eliard's sense of direction more than his own, so took the next turn as the other man chose, then nearly collided with him as he froze mid stride.

"Mother above, Eliard!" Rolph complained. "Don't just stop—"

Eliard hushed him sharply.

"I will not—"

"Shut up, Rolph," Eliard said, and the quaver in his voice stopped Rolph's next line of inquiry. Gertrude let out a low growl, her hot breath steaming the back of Rolph's neck.

Rolph leaned around the man's bulky pack to get a glimpse of whatever had spooked him, and his stomach dropped. Standing at another dead end was a minotaur. If it had been anything like the first minotaur Rolph had (inadvertently) defeated, he might not have had such a visceral reaction. But this was not the same.

The minotaur easily stood a head taller than the first he met, and unlike the original this one wore a metal cuirass on its broad torso. Its lower half was mostly bare outside of a rugged pair of trousers which cut off above the calf. It stood with its hands at rest on the butt of a long axe handle, the wicked double-bladed head of the monstrosity sitting on the ground.

"Back up," Eliard whispered and stepped back with one boot.

Rolph attempted to comply but came up short against Gertrude's massive foot which sat directly behind him. She let out a grumpy noise and didn't budge.

Rolph closed his eyes momentarily and cursed, then cast the last of his spells for the day. "*Back up*, Gertrude," he whispered to the dinosaur.

"WHAT WORRIES YOU, TINY DINOSAUR?"

Her voice, despite the fact that Rolph could tell she had tried to emulate his cautious tone, was still louder than a man talking at full volume in a busy tavern. Rolph winced.

"Who dares trespass in Linath's domain?" A confident voice boomed from the end of the corridor.

"They can talk?" Rolph asked.

"Some can," Eliard confirmed.

"Maybe—Maybe we can reason with it?"

"Stand and face me, children of men. I am your downfall, and this maze shall be your tomb!" The minotaur swung the axe up over one shoulder in emphasis.

"WHY DO YOU FEAR THIS ONE?" Gertrude asked, genuine surprise in her reptilian tone.

"Why? He's *massive!*" Rolph realized he was complaining to a giant carnivore about something less than half its size. "Can you do something about him?"

"YOU CANNOT? VERY WELL. STAND BEHIND ME."

"Don't have to tell me twice," Rolph said, then to Eliard, "Get behind her!"

The pair swiftly moved to the rear of the T-Rex, accompanied by a cry from the minotaur.

"Cowards!" He unshouldered the axe and advanced on them.

Gertrude stepped forward once and closed half the distance in her long stride. This appeared to confuse the minotaur who halted his approach. He seemed to recognize Gertrude and glared at her.

"You serve Linath, here, beast! Aid me in—"

His demand was cut short as Gertrude's maw closed over his upper half, swallowing the minotaur to the bottom of his cuirass. Blood and viscera sprayed out over her teeth and fell to the ground. She lifted the struggling body of the monster and whipped it back and forth like a cat snapping the neck of a rodent. Red mist showered Rolph, and his stomach churned uncomfortably.

Gertrude opened her mouth mid swing and flung the now limp form against the wall forming the dead end. It landed with a sickening crunch and crash of metal, then slumped to the floor motionless.

Rolph felt a familiar warmth spread through his body, though it was weaker than the times he had struck a blow against the creature he faced. Whether or not the Triad had recognized Gertrude as a member of their party, he and Eliard must be reaping some of the rewards from her efforts.

"*Crone's beard*," Eliard said, his tone full of awe.

Glancing over at Eliard, Rolph saw a new respect in his eyes as he watched Gertrude snuffle at the body. She daintily picked the lower half up in her front teeth. Rolph watched in horror as she chewed through his abdomen, leaving the armored top half on the ground. The crunch of bones and sinew accompanied her chewing and Rolph leaned over to the side to be sick.

She snaked her head around with concern in her eyes despite the blood and offal clinging to her lips. Rolph waved her back to her makeshift meal, stumbling a few feet away. If Rolph had needed a reminder that he had made a pact with an enormous killing machine, there it was. *At least she's on our side*, he thought, as he brought up the remnants of the last meal he'd eaten. Perhaps the one before that as well.

Chapter Sixteen
WE KINDA NEEDED THAT

Gertrude finished her minotaur snack relatively quickly, wiping her snout on the wall with loud scrapes until it was cleaned to her satisfaction. The queasiness in Rolph's gut, however, persisted as they backtracked to the next reasonable turn. Eliard had no such compunctions about Gertrude's diet, it seemed, and he frequently glanced back at the dinosaur with approval. Perhaps he was simply happy to have a giant carnivore protecting him, given the challenges the maze had started to throw at them.

Their next turn seemed to take them in the wrong direction, which made Rolph curse.

"That's the problem with Labyrinths," Eliard said with a sage tone. "Sometimes the path that seems to go the wrong way is actually the right one."

"Your wisdom isn't particularly encouraging," Rolph complained.

"It's not meant to be. I'm a realist, partly why I've always been a coward I suppose."

They went on without speaking for a while, Rolph contented to let Eliard lead the way. Eventually they grew tired and Rolph considered setting up camp. Exhaustion was the only real measure of time in the Labyrinth, with no sun to speak of. Instead of sleeping in the open they decided to pitch camp at an inconvenient dead end they had found two turns prior. Better to have something solid at their back in one direction at least.

Eliard set out their stew pot, to turn his conjured rations into something more palatable than the magic allowed. Rolph's spells had run dry after their encounter with the minotaur, the thought of which still made his stomach churn. With hand gestures and not a few muttered curses, Rolph convinced Gertrude to lay across the passageway. Her bulk effectively sealed them off from the rest of the maze, if imperfectly.

A small fire crackled merrily on the stone and the smoke drifted lazily into the high ceiling. No fire pit was needed in a place like this and there must have been some kind of natural air currents because the air remained clear around them. Given the enclosed nature of the maze, they assumed their fire wasn't likely to draw attention and agreed a hot meal was worth the miniscule risk.

An hour later, Rolph and Eliard sat with their legs stretched out in front of them, bowls of makeshift stew resting empty on the floor by their feet. Rolph had never been one for a pipe but suddenly longed for the simple comfort of one. He recalled his father sitting by the hearth smoking one after a family meal and his eyes clouded over with the memory.

What I wouldn't give to have that again, he thought, then turned to Eliard. "What will you do if we manage to get out of here?"

"Never set foot in the Labyrinth again, Triad take me if I'm a liar."

Rolph gave a hearty chuckle. "I'll join you in that oath. I was thinking about my father…I spent so much time feeling like I could never live up to his legacy. Now I just want to sit by the fire with him."

"I don't have to deal with that kind of pressure."

"No father to prove yourself to?"

"Nah, mine's dead," Eliard said. Rolph goggled at how casual Eliard was about it, and it must have shown on his face. "Ah, it's been years. You're lucky, him still being above the dirt. Anyway, what do you mean? I saw you splitting stone clean as could be to make all those improvements for the lizardfolk."

"That?" Rolph scoffed. "My father would have eaten that job for breakfast and then built a castle for lunch. He'd look at those gates and see every flaw, of which there were plenty, I assure you."

Eliard shrugged. "The people of Shulzuh seemed to like them fine. To answer your question, maybe I'll apprentice to be a stone mason. If you can do it, I stand a good chance." Eliard winked at Rolph, which made him laugh. "You're maudlin when you haven't slept, Rolph. Get over yourself and get some rest."

Rolph decided the man wasn't wrong and laid his bedroll out on the hard ground. The pair went about the small chores of shutting the camp down for the night, banking the coals, and deciding against setting a watch with Gertrude filling the space between them and potential threats. Rolph still had his hammer to hand, next to his bedding, because at this point he liked to believe he wasn't *that* much of an idiot.

He lay with his hands intertwined behind his head and sighed, staring at the distant ceiling beyond the reach of the dim glow of the torches that still lined the walls. "You know," he said into the silent air. "You're not as bad as I thought, Eliard…for a coward."

Eliard gave a rueful laugh. "And you're not so bad either, Rolph…for a fool."

They shared a final chuckle before lapsing into the quiet of their self-imposed night. Sleep came, followed quickly by "morning" when the pair stirred and woke Gertrude with their shuffling. She sat up and leaned against the wall with a sigh, clearly disappointed at having been disturbed.

Rolph managed to rekindle a small fire to cook some of the remaining oats they had scavenged from the delver's packs. The people of Shulzuh had kept them fed for the duration, and sent them with provisions aside, but the muzzy headed feeling in Rolph's head called for porridge.

Eliard grunted his approval as he came to sit by Rolph and wait for the grains to cook. He yawned and lifted his hands above his head, then paused at the apex of his stretch. "Something's wrong."

Rolph stirred the gruel absentmindedly. "What is?"

Eliard gestured at the passage beyond Gertrude. "We'd backtracked before resting for the night, yes?"

"Don't be stupid, of course we did."

"Then why," Eliard asked, "is our mark gone."

"What do you mean? It's not—" Rolph blinked heavily and rubbed a speck of dirt from the corner of his eye. "Mother's curse, it *is* gone."

Porridge set to the side and forgotten, Rolph and Eliard went to examine the nearby junction where they had turned to rest. There had been one of the Cleric's tell-tale Xs on the far wall, the left-hand side in the direction they had gone out in. Now? There was nothing but smooth, unblemished stone.

Gertrude swiped her tongue at the forgotten porridge, either not paying attention to their current predicament, or not caring. Rolph stepped into the tunnel, eyes searching for any of their other marks. The walls were blank.

"How much do you remember?" Rolph asked Eliard.

The cleric tapped his lips, obviously deep in thought. "I think...I remember the last three."

"Let's go," Rolph said, turning back into their camp. "We'll see how many are missing. Maybe it's a fluke."

Eliard winced. "But what could have wiped it off?"

Rolph shook his head, stuffing bedrolls into rucksacks and pulling the bowl Gertrude had licked clean from her grasp. She growled at him but let the offense pass. "How would I know? You're the adventurer." He hated the way his tone whined, like a child's.

It didn't help when Eliard didn't answer him.

The three of them set off down the tunnel system, Eliard leading the way.

There was a worried part of Rolph that wondered if he should go ahead and make sure there weren't traps afoot. And for a time, there wasn't a reason for it. Eliard remembered the next three "arrows," and when they found all of the markings wiped away, the need to check for traps became a necessity.

"What in all three names..." Eliard breathed when they'd backtracked to what should have been the fourth.

Gertrude grunted and swung her snout to the left. Rolph followed her gaze and found a familiar white chalk marking on the earthen wall. Rolph breathed a sigh of relief. "Looks like your memory isn't as keen as you thought, cleric."

Eliard pursed his lips, his eyes squinting at the familiar marking. "I guess it isn't," he muttered. Rolph ignored the disbelief in his voice. "Just...let's proceed carefully?"

Rolph shrugged. Didn't hurt anyone to test for traps as they went, even if he believed the cleric to be paranoid. The three of them followed the next few markings, and an uncomfortable sensation began to trickle up Rolph's spine. Their surroundings didn't feel familiar the further they followed the arrows through the tunnels. It wasn't until they came to a particular stone outcropping that Eliard stopped cold in his steps.

"I don't remember this," he told Rolph sternly.

Pride bubbled darkly in Rolph's chest. He wanted to refute the cleric's observation. Surely, they must have come this way. After all, that *was* his chalk. But the certainty in his voice gave him pause. "What is the alternative?" Rolph asked, echoing the question he had asked when they broke camp.

Eliard shook his head. "I genuinely don't know, but we did *not* come this way." He tapped the stone. "I would have remembered."

"Why is that?" The outcropping had a peculiar "arm" shape but was otherwise unremarkable to his gaze.

"Because it looks like Halmheir the Wicked?" Eliard cocked an eyebrow at Rolph.

The druid turned his incredulous gaze to the outcropping. "The cartoon?" he asked in bewilderment.

"The very one. My kids read them. Or did." Eliard's eyes took on a faraway look, and Rolph politely turned his gaze away toward Gertrude.

He threaded magic through the air, allowing them to talk.

"SUPPERLING, THIS IS NOT WHERE WE WERE," she huffed.

"I'm gathering that," Rolph swiped a hand over his scalp. "Do you know who—or what—could have done this?"

"I DO NOT KNOW WHAT YOU CALL THEM. THEY ARE SMALL THINGS. NOT VERY TASTY," she grumbled. "VERY QUICK TOO."

Rolph relayed this information to Eliard, who took a long moment to consider. "Miscreants. They're like goblins, but smarter. But if that was the case, we would see an occasional burrow along the wall. They're crafty, but they mostly hide away."

Gertrude huffed when Rolph translated. "THEN I WOULD NOT KNOW." There was an edge to her voice that suggested she didn't appreciate the second-guessing. She swung her head back and marched forward. "MAYBE WE WILL COME—"

A great cracking sound split the air and the huge monster froze. The floor beneath Gertrude caved beneath her great weight with a large crash and a surprised roar.

Dust kicked up in the air in a plume around her as Rolph and Eliard darted forward. The pitfall trap was just large and deep enough that it had only swallowed one of her thighs. However, she had braced her weight wrong and pitched into the side of the trap. "Are you okay?" Rolph asked as the air cleared.

"NO," Gertrude roared, trying to wiggle her body one way and another to try and extract herself from the hole. It was also the last thing he could make out before the magic slipped away from him.

Rolph pulled rope from his rucksack and threw one end of it to Eliard. "Think we can rig a harness for her, pull her out?"

Eliard looked from their rope to the dinosaur, "I sincerely doubt it. But we *can* try." Another roar thundered through Gertrude's chest, making the ground beneath their feet tremble.

"Let's do it fast, then." They threw ropes over the dinosaur's body, trying to secure it beneath her limbs. Rolph's great idea was that if they could just get it tied around her torso, they could somehow haul her up enough where she could find purchase in her scrambling.

Instead, she caught the ropes between her teeth and tore through them, wriggling out from the tie that Eliard had attempted. Rolph wanted to speak to her, to calm her down, but between the traps and his last conversation, his magic had run dry already.

"We're trying to help you," Rolph grumbled, trying to catch the rope to tie it back in place. When Gertrude's large maw snapped at him, it was a surprise. At least to Rolph, who had suddenly been displaced from the air her teeth sheared through. Eliard had grasped him around the middle and lifted him, pulling him out of her reach.

"What do you think you're doing?"

Rolph stared in disbelief at the struggling dinosaur. "I mean. We're friends?" At least, he thought they were. "I figured..."

"Friends? Are you insane? She's still a monster stuck in a hole," Eliard scowled at him. "She doesn't see anyone. She's panicking."

Gertrude roared again, trying to squeeze out of the hole and failing, and settled her jaw on the stone floor of the tunnel with a whimper.

"What should we do?" Rolph asked.

Eliard shook his head. "Not much at this point. Let's see if we can get out from here? We'll have to come back for her."

Rolph hated the idea. Eliard had been dependable up to this point for the three of them, but without Gertrude's help, could they even make it back to Shulzuh for help? Would she be okay on her own, like Eliard said?

"Look, it isn't unusual for monsters to get stuck in pitfall traps like this. Once she calms down some, she'll be able to get out on her own. She's smart. She may be out before we come back for her. And you saw how she almost got you. The beast can protect herself."

Rolph hesitated. Gertrude had been his companion since the beginning. She was his savior. Beyond that, she was the reason they were even down here this far. "Will she be alright?"

"No time to worry about that right now. We have to go before her wailing brings every monster in the vicinity down on us."

Rolph nodded, if a bit uncertainly, and moved back through the passage with Eliard. He glanced back over his shoulder one last time to find Gertrude, still flailing against the trap.

"I'm sorry," he murmured as they rounded the corner toward what he hoped was the exit. "I'll come back for you." Rolph's eyes stung with unshed tears, and he hoped his promise wasn't an empty one.

First, he had to survive.

INTERLUDE
GERTRUDE

Pain was the first thing that pierced Gertrude's surprise when the very floor betrayed her. Well, that and some of the metal spikes littering the pit she had half fallen into. She screamed and flailed, digging the barbs deeper but the agony only intensified her rage. The strange tiny dinosaur who had promised her freedom stood with outstretched hands as if his puny arms could help her. She snarled and snapped, frantic and uncaring of the damage she might inflict.

The other one, who always stank of fear, pulled her supperling away, shouting words she couldn't understand. The small one hesitated, but Gertrude's focus was on the pins gouging holes in her scales, her blood seeping out around her to the stones beneath. Her struggles grew less frequent and weaker, and when she calmed again the pair were gone. She was alone, again.

No, not truly. The malicious little creature who they had asked about. The clever, fast morsel that she had never tasted in all her time in the Labyrinth stood below the level of the broken floor, a small corridor leading out of the pit to a destination unknown. Much too small for her, but then again, this part of the Labyrinth was never for her.

It laughed in the darkness, eyes reflecting what little light there was. She growled but nothing in its posture changed as it watched her. It wasn't afraid of her, having fallen into its trap. She sighed and shifted, activating the bright points stinging her hide.

Maybe the goddess punished her, though that existential thought was almost beyond her abilities to consider. She had no mate, no children, nothing but the endless cycle of guarding the gate. The not-dinner who had promised to take her from this place had been the first living thing she had protected in her entire existence. If she understood irony, she might have hissed a lizard's laugh.

As her muscles gave out and she laid her head against the wall of the pit, she recognized this wasn't the worst pain she'd endured in her years. Gertrude would simply have to wait and eventually be reborn again into the cycle of death that was her existence. She closed her eyes, a wet bubble of blood bursting from her nose as she struggled to breathe.

Freedom had been a nice dream, at least for a while.

Chapter Seventeen
THAT'S A LOT OF TEETH

A CRACKLING FIRE DID nothing to raise Rolph's spirits. He stared into it, waiting for the pot of water to boil as Eliard bustled about their small camp outside of the entrance to the central Labyrinth. They had tumbled out of the gaping stone maw covered in scrapes and bruises, only narrowly escaping what had turned into a more elaborate trap than they expected.

Every one of their chalk marks had been removed or replaced, and as they traversed their path back both knew they couldn't rely on anything but their shoddy memories to get them back to the beginning. It wasn't safe to camp within the maze by themselves, without the bulk of a mature dinosaur to ward off would-be killers.

Apparently, the miscreant had figured that out and set a confusing course for them to fall into the deep pit which only partially contained Gertrude once she had gotten herself stuck in it. Rolph snapped a dry root in half angrily, tossing it into the fire as he went over the last few hours in his head.

They had managed to get back to the maze's entrance, somehow, though Rolph had kept his promise to Gertrude in mind. At each turn, instead of chalk, he took the chisel end of his hammer and marked a shallow X on the floor near the wall. He hoped their foes wouldn't think to check for another set of marks. He knew he had to get back to her.

A splash of water derailed his train of thought, and a hot droplet sizzled on his cheek. Rolph hastily wiped it away with a snarl. "Watch what you're doing!"

Eliard, who was tossing the last bits of conjured rations into the pot, gave him a sour look. The man stirred the pot twice then went back to sit on his bedroll. Rolph considered their flight and recognized that Eliard didn't deserve his ire. Thankfully they hadn't encountered any more of the armored, talking minotaurs, but a handful of goblins had harried them as they fled. They had barely scratched the surface of the Labyrinth's central maze, but had lost their strongest party member, and two delvers were never meant to take on a level this deep by themselves.

The cleric, beyond his skill with the lance, had done more for their escape than Rolph had ever expected. His divine spellcasting was much more powerful than any previous demonstrations, even going as far as to conjure a sword made entirely of magic. A perfect defense for the two of them as they warded off the slings and spears of the small party of monsters during their retreat.

The goblins had stopped pursuing them after the two of them managed to kill a few of them, but they also passed a decent distance, so Rolph had no way of knowing whether they were restrained geographically or had given up due to attrition and fear. He was likely to find out when they ventured back inside, but they needed some time to lick their wounds. Rolph had been out of magic before their hasty exit, and based on their seeping cuts and gashes, Eliard was dry as well or he'd have healed them both by now.

"Sorry." Rolph muttered.

"We're all a little worn out here," Eliard grumbled. "It's to be expected."

He was beginning to get sick of the scent of the dungeon delving stew. Eliard swore by it, but the conjured rations were, in a word, tasteless. Like something halfway between paper and gravel, but smelled of far too much salt than was necessary, wet dog, and surprisingly: onion?

"We shouldn't have left her alone like that."

"She'll be fine, happens all the time." Eliard ladled stew into their bowls and passed his across the way.

Rolph winced at the rations, but tucked in. "You say that, but we really could have used her back there."

Eliard frowned. "She was slowing us down."

"That was the point?" Rolph's surprise morphed into anger. "We are finding a way to get her *out* of the dungeon. Or weren't you listening?"

Eliard scoffed. "Of course I was listening. Are you hearing yourself? You want to bring a *monster* out of the *Labyrinth?*"

Fury rose in Rolph's chest. Soup forgotten, he launched himself across the space. One hand grabbed a fistful of Eliard's shirt and the other crashed into the cleric's jaw.

The man sputtered, his saliva specked with blood from a tear in his lip, but Rolph didn't pause. He was exhausted, hungry, and above all angry. Even still, his outburst was short-lived. By the third punch, his wrist strained and Eliard was looking worse for wear. Eliard shoved him off the moment the onslaught ended, swiping a hand over his busted lip and testing his jaw. "What in Liath's name do you think you're doing?"

Instead of answering, Rolph stood to retrieve his discarded rations and filled his bowl with a second helping.

"You're insane," Eliard hissed, feeling his nose.

Eliard wasn't wrong. Flying off the handle and punching someone was something Rolph would never have considered even a month ago. He shrugged. "Clean yourself up. Let's get back to Gertrude."

For some reason, Eliard didn't argue with him.

They packed up a few hours later, sharing only a few words. They had come to the unspoken agreement that Rolph had been justified in his attack, and Eliard was going to keep quiet the rest of their trip back to the dinosaur.

In the meantime, the cleric had found a shred enough of his magic to clear up his most immediate injuries, which didn't include his brand new bruised eye. They walked steadily down the tunnels, following the chiseled arrows that had thankfully remained untouched.

By the sixth arrow, they felt rather than heard the rumble start low in the ground beneath their feet. Eliard paused and bent his hand to the stone. He paled. "Back up, back up!" He hissed, shoving Rolph backwards.

"What is it?"

"She was right," Eliard managed. "Get up that outcropping."

Rolph pulled himself up on a natural ledge and helped Eliard up into the space. "What do you mean?"

Eliard shushed him and drew them back away from the edge, so they could hardly make out the floor below. "Stay down," he whispered, his voice barely above a breath.

Rolph scowled, uncertain of what could have caused the man so much fear. He opened his mouth to challenge the coward when the scratches of talons on stone raised the hair on his arms. He wiggled along his stomach so he could peer over the edge.

Small creatures and their furred bodies thundered through the corridor, swarming over the floor in such magnitude he couldn't make out the stone beneath their feet. Teeth and sharp spears flashed through the fray, and Rolph leaned forward to get a closer look when Eliard yanked him back by his collar. He shook his head and put a finger to his lips.

Rolph considered arguing with him for all of the briefest moments before he registered the genuine fear in the man's eyes. Of all the monsters they'd fought, he had never seen Eliard so frightened.

Eventually the thunder of small footsteps drifted down the corridor. Eliard waited several minutes of silence before he nodded stiffly and started climbing down.

"What were they?" Rolph asked.

"Keep your voice down," Eliard growled, helping him down from the wall. "We can't take them in our state. We couldn't take them by ourselves in our best condition."

"They looked like little kobolds," Rolph observed. Eliard had picked up his pace, and Rolph struggled to match it. "Do they really pose such a threat?"

Eliard shook his head and powered on. "Let's find your dinosaur," he grumbled. "I'm not going to argue with an idiot with porridge for brains."

"What did you call me?"

Eliard turned. "*One* of those, sure. Drop kick it into a wall, go about your day." He gestured widely, encompassing the entire tunnel. "But hundreds of them? Tell me how you might fare."

"I don't know, do they have teeth?" Rolph hazarded.

"Razor teeth. And sharp objects. We can't face them alone. We need your stupid monster."

Chapter Eighteen
THAT WILL NEVER WORK

Rolph had never seen a dead dinosaur.

He hadn't laid eyes on a live one before tumbling into the Labyrinth, but this was not a sight he wanted to check off his list. The great T-Rex's chest didn't move as Rolph stepped to the edge of the pit. Her head lolled to one side, resting against the level of the stone floor he stood on. The majority of her body had slumped into the space below, spikes showing through the thinner parts of her body. He was sure there were more, but he imagined her bulk hid them like a pincushion.

Rolph's chest tightened, and his breath came in short, sharp, gasps. He dropped to his knees and placed a hand on Gertrude's cold scales. "I wasn't sure if she'd still be here."

Eliard came up beside Rolph and placed a hand on his shoulder. "She was a mighty beast."

"How does it work?"

"Hm?" Eliard asked.

"The Labyrinth. She told me she'd been reborn countless times. How does it work? Maybe we could go wait there for a bit? Go back and get her?"

"It's not always consistent, but as far as I understand she won't be reborn until we either leave or die, then the next delvers to enter will encounter her again."

Rolph heaved a sigh and considered for a moment. "So, we're doomed."

"You and I can get out through the other gate, Rolph. I know you made a promise but she's dead now. We can go back."

A tear rolled down Rolph's cheek. He took off his pack and began fishing around in it. "Get me a rope, will you?"

"What do you need that for?"

"If we're going, I'm not leaving her like this."

"Rolph—"

"She spared me and saved my life besides. Yours too." Eliard opened his mouth to speak but Rolph raised a hand. "Maybe it's stupid, but I don't care. Help me get down into the pit; I want to remove what spikes I can."

Rolph knelt and continued removing items from his pack, placing them to the side as he searched for one of the chisels he'd taken with him from Shulzuh. Eliard gasped when Rolph set down the two potion bottles he had saved from the original party's stores. Rolph glanced over to find him staring at them.

"What? It's not like the healing potion will do anything."

"I...what? No, idiot, the other one. Where did you get it?"

Beside the red healing potion, the other iridescent bottle shimmered, its colors shifting and glittering in the light. Eliard's magic had kept Rolph from dipping into this meager apothecary, and he couldn't recall if he had ever told Eliard he possessed them still. "Your friend's packs. These were the only two bottles to survive. Why? What's this one do?"

Eliard swallowed heavily. "It's a potion of resurrection."

"I've had that on me the whole time?! Maiden's grace! I hadn't even wrapped it for safety..." Eliard stooped and attempted to snatch the potion, but Rolph was quicker and pulled it away from his grasping hand. "Don't you dare. I can use this on Gertrude."

"Now, Rolph," Eliard said, raising his hands in supplication. "Don't be hasty. We can save it for our trip out, just in case."

"For what?" Rolph's ire rose and the hair on the back of his neck stood. "For when we encounter something the two of us can't handle? Then after it kills one of us the other can bring that one back so it can do it a second time?"

Eliard frowned. "We don't even know if it works on monsters."

Rolph glared at the man. "She is no monster."

Eliard's grumpy expression deepened, but he said nothing.

"You said it yourself, I made a promise," Rolph went on. "I might not be good for much, but by the Triad, if I have a chance to keep my word I'm going to do it. Now get me a length of rope so I can get these spikes out of her. Best if we remove them before I try the potion."

Rolph tucked both potions into his pouch, well out of reach of the cleric, then secured his hammer and chisel in his belt. Eliard's face was grim, but he let out a length of rope and helped lower Rolph down into the pit. Under a controlled descent it wasn't nearly as dangerous as it would have been as a surprise.

Closer examination yielded a fuller picture for Rolph. The spikes turned out to primarily consist of old, corroded spears. A number of their hafts had shattered under Gertrude's weight without piercing her scales. What wasn't an old weapon was a long chunk of stone or metal. He stepped gingerly around the various obstacles and inspected the dinosaur's still form. A small passage led off from the pit itself, only visible from his new vantage below the floor, but now wasn't the time for exploration.

Blood had seeped from multiple wounds, and he got up close and personal with some of the spearheads that had pierced all the way through the thinnest parts of her legs. It was a gruesome sight, and Rolph's gorge rose each time he slipped in a slick pool. He worked carefully, doing his best to break the offending shards with his tools, then using his enhanced strength to pull them free of her flesh.

Rolph winced every time, even though Gertrude was beyond pain. Eliard stayed above on the solid floor, seeming to supervise after a time and call out spears Rolph had missed. Eventually the pile of sharp pointy bits far outnumbered the remaining ones Rolph couldn't reach. There was no effective way to move the dinosaur to get at anything underneath her, and he prayed the magic would take care of those few.

"How do I do this?" Rolph called up to Eliard.

"It's a potion."

Rolph closed his eyes and sucked air through his teeth in frustration. "I *know* it's a potion. But I've never fed one to a *dinosaur* before."

"Because you're not supposed to."

"If you're not going to be helpful, just say so!"

Eliard replied after a few moment's pause, "I'm not going to be helpful. This is a stupid idea."

"Fine," Rolph huffed. "I'll figure it out without you, and then I'll let Gertrude eat you when she's on her feet again."

"Fine!" Eliard cried. He fixed the loose end of his rope to an iron sconce and shimmied down to join Rolph in the pit. It was much easier going now that the mason had removed so many of the protrusions.

"Pull her jaw open," Rolph said, gesturing to the dinosaur's closed maw.

"Me? Why don't you do it and I'll feed her the potion?"

"Which do you want, to be the one on the outside holding her mouth open? Or the one putting their hand inside to pour it down her gullet?"

Eliard considered for half a second before nodding. "I'll just go pull her jaw open..."

Rolph gave a silent prayer. *Goddesses save me from cowards.*

The cleric hooked his fingers into what would count as Gertrude's lips and heaved. Her teeth parted only slightly more than a hand's breadth. Rolph gestured for him to widen the gap, but Eliard shook his head, and his arms shivered from the strain.

"Now or never," Eliard grunted.

Rolph swore, popped the top of the shimmering potion, then crammed the whole bottle into the dinosaur's mouth. He splashed some of the iridescent liquid against her tongue and threw the remainder straight toward her throat. He pulled his arm back just in time for the weight of Gertrude's head to snap her teeth shut again. Eliard cried out and shook his hands like he had caught them in a door. No blood sprayed from them, so Rolph assumed he still possessed all of his digits.

Rolph sat back on his haunches. "How long do we wait?"

Eliard stuck one offended finger in his mouth and joined him in front of the motionless creature. "No idea, I've never had to use one of these the *right* way before, let alone this."

They sat together for five minutes before Eliard stood and patted Rolph on the shoulder. "I'm not going to say I told you so, but—"

"But you told me so. I guess this means we head back."

They were two steps away from the rope when Gertrude's roar shook the room.

Chapter Nineteen

THE LION'S PAW

Gertrude struggled wildly to regain her feet. Her greatest injuries closed as he watched, but the spikes he hadn't managed to remove remained lodged in her hide. As she moved, they shifted and tore, leaking fresh blood. Rolph tried to summon his spell to speak with her, to calm her, but they hadn't rested properly before coming back into the maze. He had been in such a hurry to return that he hadn't considered he was as powerless as the day he rolled into the caverns of the Labyrinth.

No, he thought. *I'm not the same. Not anymore.*

"What are you doing standing there?" Eliard cried as he climbed the rope.

"Get clear!" Rolph yelled back, but instead of joining Eliard in his ascent, he stepped *toward* the raging dinosaur. He spoke in an even tone with his palms down in front of him, in what he hoped was a calming gesture. "Let me help you."

The eyes fixed on him were feral and uncomprehending. Gertrude finally stood on unsteady limbs, shaking her head from side to side as if to clear sleep from it. Rolph guessed that it might be necessary if he had spent time being dead but saved those thoughts for later. She didn't attack him, which he took as a positive sign, and edged forward. As his boots scraped through the rubble littering the floor, Gertrude's attention narrowed on him.

"Easy. Easy," he repeated, drawing out the word like he might soothe a horse. He was within reach of one of her haunches, where a spear protruded from a wound that would have killed a man Rolph's size. He moved to grasp it, but Gertrude swung her body around and snapped at Rolph. He dodged to the side, and she lifted her head, screaming. The sound deafened Rolph in the small space.

He circled as best he could to regain his proximity to the weapon sticking out of her skin. "I guess we do this the hard way," he muttered, then lunged for the haft. Gertrude's maw darted down again, her hot breath pouring out over Rolph as she narrowly missed biting his head off. Her aim was imperfect, but not terrible, and her teeth closed around the collar of his shirt.

Gertrude yanked Rolph upward, and the memory of her flinging half a minotaur into the air made Rolph's stomach flip even more than the forces she was applying to his torso. He maintained his grip on the spear shaft, using the momentum to rip the barb from her body. A bright spray of blood accompanied it, and she dropped Rolph to the ground as she howled in pain.

His first gambit had paid off, and he tossed the rusty weapon to the side, pulling the remaining potion out of his pouch. Rolph pulled the cork with his teeth as he rushed Gertrude. In retrospect, Rolph might have considered running headlong *toward* an enraged dinosaur to be the single dumbest choice of his entire life—thus far, anyway.

Gertrude clearly hadn't expected the small man to push his "attack", and her response was sluggish. She once more attempted to catch him in her jaws, but they closed over open air as Rolph ducked and slid the final few feet to reach her leg. *This had better work*, he prayed as he splashed the red liquid onto her gaping wound.

The T-Rex's pained cries turned into a quizzical hiss that Rolph had learned meant surprise from their time in Shulzuh. He took the opportunity and scrambled back toward the rope. Rolph had one hand on the braided line when a concerned trill came from behind him.

He turned and found Gertrude staring at him with eyes once again in focus, though full of discomfort and confusion. She tilted her head in question, a gesture he had become so familiar with these past weeks.

Rolph inhaled deeply and let out the longest sigh of relief. "Yes. It's me. Your supperling."

"How did you know the healing potion would work?" Eliard asked.

The three of them sat around a small fire among the rubble in the pit trap, Gertrude settled into a sleepy hillock against the small tunnel in the wall to block it.

Rolph and Eliard sat an arm's length apart from one another, watching the beast's chest rise and fall. She had gone to sleep immediately when they'd settled into camp. Rolph had long shaken the terror from his limbs and washed the bile from his mouth. It was a wonder he didn't need to replace his skivvies, frankly. "You've seen hurt dogs, haven't you?"

Eliard considered this for a beat. "I suppose I have."

"People aren't so different if you can forgive the metaphor," Rolph grumbled.

"Get on with it. Dogs, people, whatever."

"When animals—*and people*—are injured, they will do everything in their power to make the hurt stop. They can't tell the difference between friends and enemies. They mistake help for hurt." The stonemason shrugged. "It's the same for Gertie."

Eliard chuckled. "She's 'Gertie' now?"

Rolph smiled sheepishly. He supposed saving someone's life might earn you the right to give them a nickname. But he could never say that aloud lest Eliard, who was part of the delving party that saved his life before trying to sacrifice it, give him one. Great snores rumbled through the dinosaur's large body. They weren't going to be worth anything in a fight this evening. All of them needed rest.

"She didn't see us for anything but danger. The healing potion was just enough to bring her back to her senses."

"That doesn't work for people," Eliard scoffed. "You back a man into a corner, he's going to fight whether you give him a potion or not."

"Says the cleric who set up a human sacrifice to escape the Labyrinth." Rolph couldn't help the bitterness that threaded his words.

"It wasn't personal. You'll have to let it go sometime."

"Will I? Anyway, there are small pockets of beggars down by the river. Do you remember them?"

The city built around the Labyrinth's gaping maw was bisected by a river. Anyone who visited Mayfair would know about it.

"Sure."

"Lots of people like you don't go down there. People like me, too," Rolph admitted. "We think it's unsafe." Eliard looked at him skeptically, and Rolph continued. "A lot of them are pretty nice folk. Trouble is, they've been hurt. They're backed into corners. They're in a state of survival, like Gertrude." Rolph's eyes were getting heavy. He shrugged and turned over in his bedroll. "You have first watch?"

Eliard frowned. "Wait, you're just leaving me there? What was your point?"

"Imagine the king gave them just enough to eat, maybe roofs over their heads." Rolph shrugged, pulling the travel blanket up beneath his chin. "Suppose they wouldn't want to fight for morsels of food anymore."

"You sure you're feeling alright? You're comparing enraged dinosaurs with beggars. I've dropped coins in their cups and the feral light in their eyes only wants more."

Rolph glanced once more at Gertrude. "It'd be worth trying, though. Wouldn't it?"

When Eliard didn't reply, Rolph gave into the pull of his deep slumber.

Gertrude was the first to wake them. Rather, the rumbling of her stomach and the licking of her chops woke them. Rolph felt that he had barely blinked. His body felt a mite lighter though, and he was confident he could pull magic from the air again.

Eliard snored a few feet away from him.

Gertrude sighed and nuzzled her snout a bit closer to their camp, nudging at the coals and their packs. "Hey—*hey!*" Rolph argued, leaping to his feet. "You're gonna break something. Look, I know you're hungry. Just give me a second." Gertrude gave him an annoyed look but settled back on her haunches. She gave him a gentle trill and turned her gaze to their packs.

"I'm on it," Rolph grumbled and rifled through their equipment. There wasn't much for the massive creature to eat, but he did find some of the last strips of mushroom jerky that would at least put her off from eating one of them...for a half an hour. They really needed to get a move-on. He nudged Eliard with his boot. "Get up, let's go."

Eliard groaned something unintelligible, but sat up anyway, wiping the sleep from his eyes.

Rolph started packing their things.

"Where...going?" Eliard managed, rolling out of his bedroll.

"We have to keep moving, Gertrude needs to eat."

A skittering noise sounded from across the pit. Eliard rolled onto his feet in one swift motion, aiming his staff at the sound. Rolph frowned and scanned the area. Was it one of the miscreants they had seen the day before?

"What do they eat?" Rolph whispered.

Gertrude's eyes were fixated on a rock, her large tail lazily swaying in the air, feline-like. "I don't know," Eliard whispered. "Everything?"

"Big things?"

Eliard gave Rolph a wry look and nodded his head toward Gertrude. "Not *that* big."

Rolph considered the giant lizard. *Forget the miscreants*, he thought. Maybe it was time to reintroduce the top of the food chain. "Alright, Gertie. We're going hunting."

Chapter Twenty

AN UNLIKELY BUFFET

Trying to sneak through the tunnels with a large, hungry dinosaur was a difficult task, to put it simply. Eliard had cast a spell to make their footsteps soundless. If not for Gertrude's breathing, they may have been able to sneak closer. Instead, they gave the miscreant enough of a gap to follow its furry movements, but not so close that it would alert it to their presence.

Rolph watched its swaying footsteps and lazy tail twitches and wondered if it was injured. If it knew it was being followed, it didn't give any sign.

Its little feet pattered over the stone as it scampered through the tunnels. Rolph took a forward position in their trio, and Eliard hung back only far enough to guide Gertrude and recast any masking spells necessary to keep her hidden. It was a struggle keeping up with the creature, and Rolph found himself having to sprint occasionally so he wouldn't lose sight of it.

He turned a quick corner in hot pursuit and stopped short when the miscreant paused in its dash, then slid against the wall for a few steps before scampering back onto its original path. Curious, Rolph followed the same steps and pooled his magic forward over the spot the miscreant had avoided. Sure enough, it glowed the bright green indication it was a trap.

Even in its potentially delirious state, it appeared to have the muscle memory to dart around impending traps.

Rolph gestured to Eliard twelve feet behind him, but he didn't have time to confirm whether the cleric had understood his signal. The miscreant had bounded three lengths through the tunnel ahead and was turning a corner. Eliard wasn't a stupid man, though. He had to rely on the adventurer's prior experience on the levels above them.

Considering the fact that after the third corridor twist, he hadn't heard anything from behind him, Eliard must have registered what he was trying to convey.

Four more traps passed this way: with a rapid hand signal to the rear, a skid around a surprising dip or a hidden pressure plate, all without incident, and Rolph was beginning to gather confidence. At least until the tiny creature slipped through a crevice and disappeared from sight.

"Crone's beard," he grumbled quietly.

He stalled and waited for his heart to slow in his ears, taking deep breaths and listening. The sound of the miscreant's tiny feet had long disappeared, but maybe there was something else he could pick up on.

Once Eliard and Gertrude caught up to him a few moments later, it was clear there was nothing more to hear. The dinosaur dipped her face near Rolph's and gave him a quiet rumble of annoyance.

"I know it's not your style," he muttered. "But we're trying to get you a buffet."

She huffed and straightened. She might not have been as pleased with his answer as he'd like, but she seemed willing to let him see it through—at least for another few moments—before she rampaged.

"Where did it go?" Eliard asked, and Rolph led him to the crevice where the cleric crouched. He cocked his head and listened, like Rolph had done, and a sly smile crept over his features.

"What is it?" Rolph asked, still keeping his tone to a whisper.

"I think we let Gertrude smash this wall down."

Rolph gave him a puzzled look but then heard it too: a chorus of squeaks larger than the skittering he and Eliard had seen the day before. He pressed magic into the opening, the same way he would check for traps, and felt that it dipped about two or three feet down and took a hard left where it opened out into what he assumed was a large room.

He looked up at the Tyrannosaurus rex and gave her a smile. "Hungry?"

Gertrude's tail swayed in a universal display of pleasure.

"Like fish in a barrel. Plenty of food for her to eat." Eliard shrugged. "Plus, it will help us later on if we get rid of most of them now."

"And if they escape?"

"Then we have fewer to deal with when they regroup."

A loud grumble startled the both of them. Their gazes shot up to the dinosaur who cocked her head at them. It took a moment for Rolph to realize that the sound had been her stomach.

"Alright." Rolph pulled his hammer from his belt. "Are we supporting her from behind then?"

"You're catching on." Eliard grinned, pulling the lance from his back.

Rolph nodded at Gertrude. "Go get them."

If Gertrude's lips could peel from her sharp fangs in a smile, they would have.

With a roar she charged forward, head angled down so that it crashed through the wall. The resulting boom made Rolph wish he had covered his ears. Debris fell around them, and the surprised cries of miscreants rose in a painful chorus. Not to mention the snapping of tiny bones and the thump of monster bodies as Gertrude swiped her maw to and fro, picking up mouthfuls of the tiny creatures as she went.

"Rolph!" Eliard warned as he used the end of his spear to launch a fleeing miscreant back into the fray.

"Right!" Rolph corrected his stance and swung his hammer down on a fuzzy creature attempting to sneak past Gertrude's legs.

The room they'd burst into was flooded with miscreants, so tightly gathered that Rolph couldn't see the floor past their bodies in the midst of the chaos. The dinosaur's feet were as deadly as her hungry mouth, crushing miscreants underneath.

Someday, Rolph committed to himself as he punted another furry body back into the crowd, he would not be nauseous at the sound of snapping bones.

It only took a few horrifying moments of Gertrude's delighted feasting for some of the miscreants to turn to their weapons and mount a counter defense. Rolph, distracted with swinging miscreants back into the fray to be eaten, dimly saw three lines of furry creatures gathering at the edge of the room from the corner of his eye. Silver metal glinted in their hands. "Gertrude!" He shouted a warning, but his voice was lost in the wet crunching of her breakfast.

She hadn't seemed to hear him, continuing to wreak her havoc. Rolph edged his way into the room, leaving Eliard the task of covering their exit on his own. The first spear was thrown before Rolph could get close enough to warn her again. She didn't notice the first pinprick of metal. The tiny weapons looked like thin sewing needles in her thick hide. Another struck her side, then the third, fourth, fifth, all in rapid succession embedded themselves in her skin.

Gertrude roared, sounding more annoyed to Rolph's unmagicked ear than in true pain. He hefted his hammer and charged into the lines. Sharp pain sliced his skin as some of the miscreants directed their attention to the human charging into them, but he was able to catch most of them unaware long enough for Gertrude to stomp her way into them.

Rolph paused to catch his breath while Gertrude stomped and chewed her way through the rest of the crowd—except there weren't many miscreants left to call it a proper crowd. The entire room was awash in red viscera. Gertrude gleefully chased down a few stragglers while Eliard shuffled into the room and Rolph surveyed the grotesque scene. A frantic squeaking caught his attention where Gertrude had trapped three miscreants in a hollow in the wall. She growled, trying to jam her maw into the space, taloned fingers grasping at air in frustration.

Eliard caught Rolph's eye and nodded. They joined her as she snapped up a leg of one, throwing back her head and gulping it down in one go. One of the furry miscreants bolted, taking advantage of the gap, but Eliard caught it and flung it into Gertrude's eager mouth. She swallowed it gratefully, large tail swaying in pleasure while Rolph forced down his own bile.

The final miscreant tucked itself against the wall, tiny chest heaving and legs trembling. Gertrude bent her head again to terrorize it, but Eliard gestured for her to wait.

"The other one helped us find this place, they know how to navigate the traps. Let's take this one?"

It wasn't a terrible idea. He bent to the miscreant. Its small, furry body and shining eyes might have looked cute, if he didn't now know what they were capable of. It moved to scamper away from him, but Gertrude snapped her jaws at it, startling it back to Rolph. Eliard passed him some rope.

Rolph gestured at it with the coil. "I'm gonna tie you using this for now," he explained. Eliard scoffed behind him, but he ignored the cleric. "If you help me and my friends, I'll let you go. Otherwise..." He nodded at the dinosaur who let loose an intimidating rumble.

The tiny creature seemed to take the threat seriously, considering it didn't try to flee again while he tied the length of rope around it, leaving some slack to use as a makeshift "leash."

"Okay." Rolph nodded to himself. "Let's get a move on, then."

Chapter Twenty-One

"HIRED" HELP

Rolph was elated by their success. Capturing one of the remaining monsters had been a means to an end. The creatures were smart, agile, and could lead them to the center of the Labyrinth avoiding any more dangers.

Or so he assumed.

First, they ended up back at the pit trap where Gertrude had fallen. It gibbered words neither of the delvers understood and pointed downward. Gertrude only glared at the creature like a forgotten chicken wing left on a plate, licking her lips periodically. It was unnerving to more than their prisoner. Eliard turned a bit green at the sight, likely at the memory of her frenzy from earlier.

"I don't know what you mean," Rolph said slowly, enunciating every word like he was speaking to a child.

The miscreant made walking motions with its fingers and pointed below, again. Rolph narrowed his gaze, eventually picking out the tunnel he had found when they had rescued Gertrude from the pit.

"We can't go that way!" Rolph raised his hands in exasperation, waving at Gertrude. "She won't fit." He held his arms wide and shook his head. "TOO BIG."

The creature cocked its head and waited.

"Maybe we should let her eat it," Eliard muttered, gesturing at the dinosaur.

Catching the motion, if not the words, the creature yelped and cowered, wrapping its arms around itself.

"Oh, you understand *that* do you?" Rolph complained and pointed behind them. "FIND ANOTHER WAY."

The miscreant bowed and scraped its hands against the floor, moving back the way they came. Rolph shared a look with Eliard, but he had no better plan than the one he'd come up with.

It wasn't all bad news, once they started moving in what felt like a "right" direction. After passing the entrance for hopefully the last time, the creature warned them about three different traps which they navigated successfully. One was another large pit trap, which Gertrude whined anxiously about until the miscreant took them through an alternate route large enough for the predator.

After a few more hours of this, Eliard's patience had worn thin. They encountered a handful of additional traps and more than one misunderstanding that left everyone slightly singed and vaguely worse for wear.

"Move!" Eliard bellowed, pushing a booted foot against the backside of the hairy creature who walked ahead of them. It stumbled and hissed, falling onto its side to avoid crashing onto its bound wrists. The long lead remained tied to Eliard's belt. He had insisted, barring attaching the thing to Gertrude's leg, that he was the best candidate to keep it from running away.

Rolph didn't like the change in the lancer, who seemed to take more delight in the miscreant's suffering at their hands after each turn of the path. "Let's take a break, we've been walking forever."

Eliard shot Rolph a stare but nodded gruffly. They turned into yet another dead end after expending one of Rolph's few spells and set up camp. This time Eliard *did* tie their prisoner's leash to Gertrude's leg like he was leaving a horse outside the tavern. The dinosaur wasn't much help when it came to human needs like rest and food, but she made an excellent hitching post.

In short order they had a pot of delver stew simmering. Rolph glanced over and the miscreant's nose twitched, drool pooling in the corner of its mouth. Perhaps there was a way to encourage their captive's participation without Eliard's slings and arrows. When the soup was as ready as it ever was, Rolph ladled out a bowl of it and walked slowly over to their prisoner.

"What do I call you?" he asked, settling onto his haunches in a crouch. Rolph wasn't a tall man, but he towered over the miscreant when standing. "My name is Rolph."

The hairy thing cocked its head again in a listening gesture but said nothing. Rolph set the bowl on the ground and pushed it gently toward the creature. As he stepped back it darted forward and scooped up the dish, pouring the hot liquid greedily into its mouth. Seemingly oblivious to the scalding temperature, it sucked down the mixture, chewing and slurping loudly. The carnage was over quickly, and it sat on the bare earth with a belch, picking at its razor-sharp teeth with a small claw.

Rolph stuck a thumb in his chest. "Rolph." The miscreant's eyes focused on his gesture, so he repeated it. "Rolph."

Its hands were small, gnarled things, but it took its own thumb and pointed at itself. "D'zrt," it said in a guttural tongue.

"Dessert?" Eliard howled with laughter. The man was apparently done with his dinner and had come up behind Rolph. "That's what it's going to be if it's not more useful."

Rolph sighed and shooed Eliard away. He went, chuckling and talking to himself about giving his left leg for a piece of pie.

The mason pointed at the miscreant and attempted to mimic its tone. "D'zrt."

Its eyes lit up and it bobbed its head excitedly. Then, it pointed at the mason and croaked, "R'lf."

"Close enough, yes," he said with a chuckle. "Look, if you help us and get us to the center of the Labyrinth? I'll let you go free."

It stared at him with guileless, uncomprehending eyes.

Rolph sighed. "Well, it was worth a try."

Despite Rolph's misgivings, the next "day" went smoother. He found D'zrt curled up against Gertrude's foot, the lead still tightly knotted and no gnawed frays in the rope. In fact, the miscreant seemed excited to see the mason. It jumped to its feet once alerted to Rolph's approach and had an eager gleam in its eye.

They struck camp in short order and their captive set off in a confident direction at as brisk a pace as its lead would allow. Rolph raised an eyebrow at Eliard, who shrugged but didn't argue against the positive development. The miscreant did a much better job at pointing out pressure plates and other challenges on their path, and their speed of travel increased significantly from the day before.

"At this rate, we'll hit the center in no time," Rolph commented to Eliard after they had taken a break for some mushroom jerky. He shared a piece of it with D'zrt, who stuffed it into its mouth in one bite. "GOOD JOB." He reached out hesitantly to pat the creature on the head, but it snapped its jaws shut inches shy of Rolph's fingers with a shrewd look. Rolph jerked his hand back, and the placid expression returned to D'zrt's face as he chewed. *Noted*, he thought.

Their travel continued with D'zrt's willingness to actively aid their path unabated. Without any kind of map, they had no way to know how far they had gone or how much farther they would need to go. The language barrier between them and the miscreant also meant they had to trust it, which Eliard kept making grumbling noises about, but Rolph didn't see any other option. The promise of freedom, as much as it understood their conversation from the day before, seemed to have whet its appetite enough to help in good faith.

Right, left, straight, ramp up, slope down, the twists and turns grew incredibly convoluted. Rolph continued marking their path with the chisel end of his hammer, and they had managed to not cross their own path in the last day and a half. Rolph's stomach rumbled, indicating they had been walking long enough to warrant another meal, when the corridor ended in a large chamber. The walls were similar to the rest of the maze, but the scale of the room was immense compared to what they had experienced thus far.

Rolph gave a low whistle, which echoed strangely in the open space. D'zrt bounded back and forth like a dog on a leash, beckoning them to follow it toward the center of the room. Where they entered was an open archway, with one massive door on the far side of the chamber across from them. The walls to either side held no portals but bore bas relief carvings he couldn't make out at that distance.

The floor was also patterned either with massive stone tiles, or lines cut into the rock itself. Rolph's professional curiosity almost got the better of him as he stooped to examine one of them, reaching out a hand to determine the method of construction. A hand grabbed the back of his shirt, and the brush of sharp claws told him it was D'zrt who pulled him backwards with a squeak.

He fell on his rump and twisted around, catching the frantic shaking of D'zrt's head. The miscreant let his shirt go when Eliard jerked on the lead and pulled it back, making the creature stumble and fall to the ground itself.

"What was that about?" Rolph asked, exasperated.

D'zrt clumsily got to its knees and groveled, pointing at the edge of the tile Rolph had been about to touch. It shook its head again, violently.

"Is it a trap?" Rolph asked, but the blank stare D'zrt gave him made him curse. Instead of trying again, he pulled his thumb across his throat and lolled his head to one side with his tongue sticking out.

D'zrt nodded excitedly and pointed at the stone again.

"Well, I'll be damned," Eliard said.

Rolph rolled onto his knees and stared at the small creature. "Thank you, D'zrt." He fixed his gaze on Eliard. "See? It's helping us. We can trust it."

Eliard huffed, but nodded solemnly, letting the lead go slack between him and the creature.

The miscreant didn't reply but instead got to its feet and pulled Eliard by the lead toward the center of the room. The men followed, their boots making heavy footfalls which echoed in the silence of the chamber.

The pattern in the stone changed near the middle and a wide circle had been scribed, separated into three sections. Perhaps a nod to the Triad, but it was too simple geometry to make more than an educated guess at the intention of the creator.

D'zrt scrambled across the wide tile and beckoned them to follow him. Rolph stepped into the circle, followed by Eliard, and then Gertrude. When the dinosaur's foot pressed her whole weight downward a grinding sound filled the air and the section of floor they had trod on sunk with a "click."

Rolph's eyes widened in surprise and D'zrt turned to glare at the party. Its eyes were no longer friendly, but full of malice. Its lips curled in a feral grin, showing their sharp teeth.

"You fools."

Chapter Twenty-Two

THERE ARE TWO OF THEM?!

Rolph gaped at the words coming out of D'zrt's mouth. "You can talk?"

D'zrt stood straight for the first time since they had encountered it, adding inches to its still diminutive height. It scoffed. "Of course I speak the common tongue."

"But—I thought—we…" Rolph lost the ability to speak, his words running into each other as he wrapped his mind around what had just happened.

"You believed what you wanted to believe, human." D'zrt sneered at him. "That I was lesser, and you would be my master. How does it feel to know I was in control the whole time?"

Eliard laughed. "Told you so."

Their repartee was interrupted by another noise, the ugly grinding of stone sliding on stone. Rolph nearly snapped his own neck with how fast he looked over his shoulder to witness an enormous slab of rock descending from the ceiling of the arch they had entered by. He turned and lifted a hand as if he could stop its descent, but Rolph hadn't made a single step toward the exit when it closed with a crash of finality.

"Now," D'zrt said, a chuckle bubbling up from his chest, "you will face your doom. You—"

Gertrude ducked and swung her head at D'zrt with impressive and surprising speed, flinging the creature until it crashed against the ceiling. They watched as it completed its painful arc and landed with a wet splat against the ground. Gertrude narrowed her eyes and stalked over to lick at the crumpled body of the miscreant.

"Gertrude!" Rolph cried. She paused only to glance in his direction, then took the entire body in her mouth, swallowing after barely a chew.

"He was dessert after all," Eliard mocked.

Rolph's horror was short lived as the three sections of floor inched downward, forming a circular pit in the center of the room. Gertrude had already moved off, to chase after her bloody morsel, but Eliard and Rolph jumped from the platform as it descended. They stood at the edge, peering down the growing depression. In addition to the scraping of stone, a low chittering joined the undercurrents of sound.

Eventually the edges of the tiles exposed dark openings in the sides of the pit, reminding Rolph of a cistern where water might flow. Instead of a rush of water, however, mandibles poked out of the tunnels before enough had been exposed to let their owners show their full forms.

"Cave crawlers!" Rolph cried, taking a bigger step back from the edge as the insectoid creatures revealed themselves. They ran with swift legs across and around the stone circle without climbing them, mixed in size from two hand-spans to nearly Rolph's height in length. None appeared to be the adults like what they had faced earlier in the open caverns, but the mass of writhing monsters sent chills down Rolph's spine.

Gertrude took two large steps toward the pit and peered over the edge. A massive belch washed a wave of stench past Rolph and Gertrude followed it with a hacking noise, finally coughing up one of D'zrt's arms which fell limply into the swirling mass. Rolph winced as adolescent cave crawlers reduced the remnant of their captive to bits in moments.

"What now?" Rolph asked Eliard, who was scanning the room.

"We wait. There's no point in running around with our heads cut off, we're as likely to fall into the next part of the trap." Recovering Gertrude and hunting the miscreants seemed to have put some steel into Eliard's spine.

Glancing around the chamber, Rolph waited for the worst. Maybe the walls would start pressing inward. Perhaps the rest of the tiles were set to fall in an intricate trap. The mystery solved itself when the enormous door on the far side of the room cracked open with a boom. Even more surprising than the sound was what followed as the horned head of another dinosaur pressed quickly into the chamber.

"You're joking." Eliard laughed uncomfortably.

In another life, Rolph might have considered himself blessed. Seeing not one, but two different dinosaurs was beyond his wildest imaginings. This one didn't have the same razor-sharp teeth as Gertrude but had a wickedly sharp beak with a horn above it. Its head bore a wide plated crest larger than any shield he had ever seen, two more horns curving out from its forehead. Attached to those two bony protrusions were leather leads similar to what he would have found on a horse-drawn wagon.

Stranger still was the figure who rode upon its back, holding the reins. Larger than the miscreant by far, the creature astride the unfamiliar dinosaur had a husky build. Its leathery skin was tight over heavily muscled arms and chest. It bore a wide bladed battle axe across its back, strapped to a crude harness, and as Rolph's examination traveled upward he took in the tusks protruding from the creature's misshapen face.

Once fully inside the room the rider twitched the reins and the dinosaur turned to shove its head against one side of the door then the other, slamming them shut. The creature turned again and shook itself in an oddly horse-like gesture, stamping one foot in front of itself.

"Hobgoblin," Eliard spat. "Riding a...triceratops? Linath's tears, this day is getting weirder."

Rolph could only nod in mute agreement. The danger was clear to him, now. The broad triceratops appeared poised to chase unwary delvers who sprung their trap into the mass of crawlers. Most likely effective, and deadly, based on their calm demeanor.

He knew nothing of either creature, only having recalled Gertrude's species from its fame. "Now would be a good time to fill me in, Eliard."

The triceratops scraped a giant foot against the ground like a bull preparing to charge. The hobgoblin flexed its scarred shoulders and pulled its axe free from its sheath. It waved the weapon over its head in a wide circle, whooping and kicking its mount's flanks.

"You think I've fought a dinosaur before?!" Eliard yelled without taking his eyes off the massive creature and its rider.

"How am I supposed to know? You're the delver!" Rolph screamed in reply.

"Split up!" was all Rolph received in explanation and Eliard darted in a straight line away from Rolph.

The mason spat a curse and ran in the opposite direction. There was only one of their enemies, so long as the rider didn't dismount, so it made sense to Rolph not to group together. He cast his communication spell on the fly, the magic flowing from him and to Gertrude.

Rolph's chest heaved as he tried to speak and run at the same time. "What can you do about that thing?"

"MY COUSIN IS STUBBORN, BUT I WILL FIGHT HIM IF I MUST. I DO NOT LIKE THE THING ON HIS BACK."

Gertrude easily kept pace with Rolph, her long strides eating up ground.

"Fat lot of good I can do about it now!" Rolph glanced back and the rider had angled toward Eliard, ignoring the larger prey in favor of singling out the cleric now that Gertrude had chosen a path.

Rolph was reminded again that Eliard wasn't as useless as he had appeared when a ghostly blade materialized between him and his pursuer. The triceratops took the slashes in stride, the spectral weapon barely nicking its thick hide. The hobgoblin, however, swung its axe in fast arcs to fend off the incoming strikes. Their pace slowed, dealing with the counter-offensive, but only slightly. They still bore down on Eliard, clearly having experience fighting a moving battle.

"Can you charge it while it's distracted?" Rolph stopped to rest his hands on his knees. More running wasn't going to put him in a better position as he neared the wall.

"I WILL DO MY BEST, SUPPERLING," Gertrude replied, orienting herself to make her own beeline for the pair. She roared, lumbering into a run at her "cousin".

Rolph panted, exhaustion already threatening to overtake him for a brief moment. The crash of steel on steel and Gertrude's cries pushed adrenaline into his blood and drew his eyes wide open again. He pulled his hammer from his belt, considering his options.

None of them looked good.

Eliard wasn't holding his own so much as staving off the inevitable, unless something changed in their situation. If he stayed out of the fray, he would make what could be a three-on-two fight into an even match, if you could call Eliard and Gertrude against the rider and his mount even. The T-Rex could likely hold her own, but the hobgoblin's skill in mounted combat likely made up for the fact that they were a combined target.

As if to prove Rolph's assumptions, the rider's axe flashed out and sliced a gouge in Gertrude's nose as she approached, head low to grab one of the triceratops' legs. She bellowed in outrage and veered to the side, moving out of range.

The triceratops shook their armored frill, and its long horns parried the strikes of Eliard's ghostly blade. The cleric stood his ground, long spear held in a high guard with the point trained on the mount. He feinted in and out, lunging in an attempt to pierce one of the monster's eyes. To Rolph's dismay, the spear point did more skittering along the bony plates than stabbing.

Gertrude had reversed course, coming up behind the triceratops and snapping at its tail. The beast was quicker than its size would have indicated, and it danced nimbly to the side. He had to do something, and quickly, or Eliard would be overwhelmed.

"Hey! You!" Rolph yelled eyes wide with surprise at his own voice. Whatever plan was half-formed in the back of his mind hadn't been communicated to the rest of his brain as he strode forward, back toward the hobgoblin. His limbs weren't his own and the cocktail of nerves coursing through his body sent energetic pulses through his extremities.

The hobgoblin spared him a glance, though his mount remained engaged with Eliard's spear work. It pointed its massive axe at Rolph with one hand. "You're next, little man." Its voice was like air through a pile of gravel, despite being the common tongue.

"Why—uh—why not now? Hm?" He continued walking, placing himself nearly where they had started. He stood near the edge of the central pit, and his stomach churned at the slithering behind him. He raised his hammer in salute, trying to quell the shaking in his hand. "Are you a coward?"

The hobgoblin screamed in outrage. "You dare insult me?! Your friends will watch you die!" He kicked his mount hard with his heels, and the creature turned immediately to face Rolph. Eliard's blade scored a slight hit or two before winking out of existence, and his spear fared little better as his foe ignored him to charge in Rolph's direction.

Rolph, both pleased and horrified that his distraction had worked, set his feet and drew his hammer back. The feet of the triceratops ate up ground between them and quickly grew closer than Rolph was comfortable with. The mason trained his eyes on the beast's cadence, and as its forward foot fell at the right time, he hurled his hammer at its lead leg. What had once worked against a charging minotaur by accident, Rolph intended to recreate with purpose.

Time slowed as the tool arced through the air, tumbling end over end until it smacked head-first into the dinosaur's ankle. He raised his hand in triumph, but his short-lived celebration ended in terror as...nothing happened. Well, not nothing. The dinosaur stopped short, about ten feet from Rolph, and cocked its head to peer quizzically at its foot. It looked down at Rolph as if to say, "Really?" Even with his enhanced strength, he was no true engineer and hadn't considered the difficulty in knocking a four-legged creature off balance.

The hobgoblin's laugh was harsh. "What did you think that would do? Now, you die, human."

Rolph's foe whistled and the triceratops stepped forward then reared back on its hind legs. Eliard and Gertrude were still too far away to do anything about the tonnage about to fall on Rolph's head, though his distraction had worked to allow them to approach from behind.

Rolph knelt and curled his arms over his head, as if shielding himself from a winter hail instead of a falling avalanche of flesh and bone. "Triad, protect me!" Rolph cried and in the intervening moment between his final prayer, and the impact of feet the size of dinner platters, *something* answered.

The energy permeating Rolph's body surged outward, and dark woody vines formed a protective sphere around him. The triceratops landed its front feet on his thorny shield, a surprised sound escaping its beak. Small cracks formed in the material, and he dove out of a wide opening in the magical brambles before it collapsed under the weight of its assailant.

The hobgoblin cursed in its native tongue, but Rolph interpreted it based on tone alone. He didn't like being thwarted at the last minute and raised his battle axe to swing down upon Rolph.

That was the moment Gertrude's massive jaws closed on the triceratops' frill. As far as damage went, the bite did less than Rolph would have expected. Instead, what she achieved was *leverage*. Gertrude shook her opponent like a dog's toy and snapped its head downward, launching the hobgoblin over the pommel of its saddle.

Rolph wasn't so lucky that the momentum carried it into the pit, but the hobgoblin landed in a heap a few feet to his left. The mason, unarmed, lunged to recover his hammer but received a glancing blow from a giant foot instead. The blow left him reeling and unable to breathe. Rolph stumbled backward, not wanting to think about what a more direct hit would have done. The triceratops squealed in anger, bucking against Gertrude's hold and goring her with one of its horns as it twisted in her grip.

Eliard, not one to miss an opportunity to kick something while it was down, struck at the prone hobgoblin with his lance. The tip pierced the thing's mid-section, and it cried out in pain. It rolled backward and clambered to its feet, one hand holding its guts in place and the other waving the battle axe in a warding gesture.

"GET DOWN!" came the garbled voice of Gertrude.

Eliard and Rolph hit the floor at once, and wind rushed over their heads as the body of the smaller dinosaur passed directly above them. Gertrude swung the beast in a wide arc, colliding with the hobgoblin and sending it tumbling into the cistern of crawlers. Gertrude released her hold and the triceratops' trajectory took it to the side of the pit without following its master in, where it sprawled limply.

The wet squelch of pincers disassembling flesh from bone reached their ears before the screams did.

Chapter Twenty-Three

Rest Here, Weary Traveler

Gertrude's breath heaved and a wound in her side pulsed with blood, slicking the floor in red. Rolph tried to suck in air, but his lungs didn't respond. Eliard was the only one of the three who appeared uninjured, and he stood dumbly with his eyes fixed on the writhing mass of cave crawlers. At least the hideous noises from below didn't last long.

The triceratops lay on the stone, glaring at them all but unwilling to stand. Between losing its rider and Gertrude tossing it across the room, it must have chosen to nurse its wounds for the moment. That worked for Rolph, because he was about to pass out.

"El—iard," Rolph croaked.

"What? Oh, hell, you're turning blue."

"Can't...breathe..."

Eliard leaped to Rolph's side and laid his hand on the man's chest. A soft glow accompanied the muttered words of his prayers, and the pain in Rolph's torso eased.

Rolph sucked in a grateful lung full of air then rushed to Gertrude's side. "Eliard, you need to heal her!"

Eliard jogged dutifully over to examine her injuries. He clucked his tongue, almost reaching out to prod at the wound but stopping when Gertrude let out a warning growl. He turned to Rolph, shaking his head. "Can you get her to stand still long enough for me to bind it? My magic is spent after all that."

Rolph could sense he had a tiny amount of magical reserves, and he focused on casting his first spell for the last time before they had a chance to rest.

Gertrude had turned to roar at the triceratops, who cast its gaze to the floor in submission. "ROOOOARRRAAND ANOTHER THING, WHAT DID YOU THINK YOU WERE DOING CHALLENGING ME—"

"Gertrude!" Rolph screamed, interrupting the tirade she had aimed at her "cousin".

"I AM VERY ANGRY, SUPPERLING. HE *HURT* ME, WHICH WAS HONESTLY SURPRISING…"

"Please stand still while Eliard binds your wound, we need to find a place to rest."

She did as Rolph asked, sitting back on her haunches and allowing Eliard to take a large cloth and hold it to her side. The triceratops lowed at the T-Rex in what sounded like confusion.

"THEY SERVE ME, COUSIN."

Rolph didn't bother translating for Eliard, who would have had a conniption. He would let that bit of fiction slide, though a part of him considered whether it was more accurate than he wanted to admit.

The other dinosaur snorted and shook its head in a gesture similar to human surprise. It continued its low honking speech.

"I WILL LET YOU RETURN TO YOUR HOME IF YOU TAKE US THERE."

Trike, because Rolph couldn't keep thinking of it as "the triceratops", blew a snort of ascent, rising shakily to its feet.

"Gertrude," Rolph continued. "We won't be able to speak for long, but when we get wherever Trike is taking us, we're going to rest until we can heal you properly. Understand?"

"OF COURSE I UNDERSTAND," Gertrude huffed, blowing a breath of hot air into Rolph's face. "TRIKE? THAT IS RIDICULOUS, BUT GOOD ENOUGH. HIS NAME IS TOO LONG AND CUMBERSOME FOR YOUR CLUMSY HUMAN LIPS."

"Clumsy? You're kidding me, I..." Rolph's complaints fell on deaf ears as Trike trundled toward the huge doors he and his rider had slammed shut earlier, with Gertrude and Eliard in tow.

Gertrude's bleeding had slowed from Eliard's ministrations, but she winced when she attempted to shove her head against one side of the doors. She growled at Trike, who hooked his horns into convenient rings set into the iron at the height of its head. Slowly, he dragged one side open, allowing Gertrude to wedge herself into position to push the other half.

Rolph stepped over the threshold and what was on the other side took his breath away. It was another vast chamber, though perhaps less than half the size of the trap behind them. Instead of bare stone, it was lush and vibrant. Rolph had never seen a real oasis, the desert being far from Mayfair, but he had read stories about them and this place fit the bill.

A pool big enough for the triceratops bubbled merrily in the center of the room, surrounded by dense mossy growth, fed by a small stream coming through a break in the wall. The greenery was lighter in color than the kind Rolph found and occasionally napped on in the forest, somewhere between a light green and gray. Instead of torches, the hall was lit with cheery metal lanterns pierced with a myriad of designs.

Trike lumbered toward a far corner, which resembled nothing less than an enormous stall Rolph might have found in any well-appointed stable. Straw was piled high around a central depression that was more nest than bed. Trike dunked his head firmly into a trough of water and drank greedily until the level had visibly gone down. Once his thirst had been slaked, he picked a mouthful of straw out of a separate bin and went to curl up in the center of the mound.

He paid them all little heed as he spun a slow circle before laying down. Loud snores quickly joined the small noises in the background of the room. Gertrude followed and drank greedily, earning a raised eyelid from Trike but no outward protest.

Rolph examined the gate they had passed through, and a large lever caught his eye, set into a mechanism in the floor. From the look of things, this appeared as much sanctum for Trike and his missing rider as anything else. Rolph made a snap judgement and pulled the lever, despite Eliard jumping forward to try and stop him. He was too late, though, and Rolph cringed in the intervening seconds before the doors swung slowly shut of their own accord.

"You lucky idiot," Eliard complained, wiping cold sweat from his brow. "Don't you *ever* pull a lever like that again before telling me. Lost a good man in a delve one time, pulling stupid stunts like that."

"Seemed like the only safe place to do it," Rolph countered. "Where are we?"

Gertrude turned at their speech, but as his spell had run out it was only a gesture of curiosity. She walked the perimeter of the room, investigating the nooks and crannies, while Rolph and Eliard approached the pool.

"I'm not sure, I suppose it's where that hobgoblin lived. A bit posh for his kind, I'll admit." Eliard gazed wistfully at the water. "What I wouldn't give for a hot bath, right now."

Rolph squinted at the bubbles rising to the top. The small stream from the far wall fed the basin, which passed out a similar crack in the other side. So, if the water replenished from one side and flowed out the other, he couldn't discern what made the bubbles.

Unless...Rolph stuck a finger into the pool and nearly cried at how warm the water was. "Eliard, I think you get your wish."

"Maiden's tears, you're kidding?" He shoved his arm in up to the elbow, ignoring how wet his clothes got. He brought it out and ran his dripping fingers through his hair, whooping with joy.

It took all of a minute for their clothes and gear to end up in a pile, minus their smallclothes, and the two men sank with exaggerated noises into the heat of the pool. Rolph breathed deeply, the moist air coating his lungs and filling him with a sense of peace he hadn't experienced since setting one toe in the Labyrinth. Even the baths at Shulzuh couldn't hold a candle to this place. He let his arms float lazily, examining his extremities as they pruned.

Eliard's spell hadn't healed him completely from Trike's attack and Rolph's eyes widened as a cut on his forearm sealed itself, then faded to a light pink scar. "Eliard..."

The older man's eyes were closed; his head leaned back against the edge of the pool. "Now is not the time to bother me," he said groggily.

Rolph stood and peered at the bottom, below where the bubbles rose from. He held his breath and ducked under the surface to get a better look. A cobalt glow pulsed from a small gem set into the base of the stone lining the basin. He broke above the water and liquid streamed down his grinning face. "Eliard! This is a *healing* pool!"

"By the Mother," he whispered, checking himself and seeming to find the same results Rolph had with his smaller injuries. He dove to perform the same investigation as Rolph, but the mason had other priorities.

"Gertrude!" Rolph cried and the dinosaur perked up from where she had laid on a large patch of moss. She walked slowly over to them, her gored side clearly paining her. Rolph splashed her excitedly, throwing water out of the pool with abandon, but other than a now slightly soggy dinosaur she seemed just as worse for wear.

Eliard surfaced in time for Rolph to grab him by the arm and pull him toward the edge. "We have to get out!"

"My first moment of happiness in two years, and you're ruining it," Eliard grumbled, but complied with Rolph's insistence.

"You'll get another chance," Rolph promised. "Gertrude, get in the pool." She didn't respond to his words other than with a tilt of her head. Rolph smacked himself on the forehead, then pantomimed sitting and pointed at the water.

Gertrude seemed to get the hint and gingerly dipped a toe into the water. Apparently, it was all the convincing she needed, because in half a heartbeat a short tidal wave slammed into Rolph and Eliard's shins, nearly knocking them off their feet.

The T-Rex sighed and trilled happily, not arguing as both Rolph and Eliard rejoined her in the water. Rolph waded over to inspect her side and found the large wound already closing. The bath continued far longer than any normal person would have tolerated, but it had been a long time coming.

"Things might be looking up," Rolph said.

Eliard groaned. "You shouldn't have said that..."

"Why..." Rolph started to ask, but his gaze traveled to the far wall where a dark portal he hadn't noticed before broke the stone expanse.

He hoped he hadn't jinxed them, but only time would tell.

Chapter Twenty-Four

A Coward's Dilemma

Despite the appearance of the portal, they didn't cut their baths short. If they were going to die, they would milk every last drop of enjoyment beforehand. In fact, both men stared at the opening for a solid five minutes just to make sure nothing popped out at them. Once satisfied, they lingered until their skin was uncomfortably wrinkled. As if creeping toward an unpleasant fate, they slowly donned their garments and shouldered their equipment.

"What do you think it is?" Eliard asked.

"Well, I'd hope we'd have noticed if it was there when we walked in since it's big enough to fit Gertrude through. So, it might be the path to the rest of the maze, triggered by something we did here. Despite how my ribs hurt, that didn't feel like the guardian we were looking for. There's also no gate out, like near where we found Gertrude." Rolph buckled the chest strap of his pack and clapped Eliard on the shoulder. "But if something was going to pop out of it and murder us, it probably would have done it while we were in our skivvies." He strode toward the gigantic archway in the wall without pausing at the threshold for more than a moment to examine the carving at its edge.

"It's the lever all over again!" Eliard cried in dismay from behind. "It's like you've learned nothing!" Grumbling and the clatter of the man snatching his spear off the ground followed Rolph, Gertrude's loud steps padding in behind him. Eliard collided with Rolph's back, where he had stopped only a couple feet into the next room. "What are you doing stopping like—" His words cut off abruptly as he apparently took in what Rolph had already seen.

Instead of an extension of the manicured oasis they stepped into a crystalline cave. Rolph had once held a cracked geode and the way light scintillated within colored stone had fascinated him. This was much the same, and his mouth fell open in awe. Despite the splashes of light from luminescent fungus reflecting in the gorgeous spines of crystal, the room itself had a monkish austerity.

The floor was flat and clean, if rough. The crystal formations sat in triplets on the white quartz floor, spaced relatively evenly. It didn't take much light to fully illuminate the bone-white room, and it shone like a pearl. It struck Rolph as closer to a church than a cave.

"The Triad," he whispered, and his words echoed strangely in the rocky chapel. Eliard said nothing but walked silently beside him. Larger than the church in Mayfair, this annex seemed an odd offshoot from the Labyrinth, like nothing they'd seen on their journey so far.

At the far end of the space were two asymmetrical doorways. As Rolph got closer, they resolved into a large door on the right, and a smaller solid mass of black stone, incongruous with the rest of the architecture, on the left. The door was large enough for Gertrude to fit through, if perhaps a tight squeeze, but the other obsidian slab was fit for a man alone.

"What is this?" Eliard asked.

"Wish I knew," Rolph replied.

Between the portals sat a stone table, upon which two crystals protruded from the surface. Similar to the portals, the left was black like the deepest onyx while the right was an opal reflecting all the colors present in the room.

"Wait, there's something inscribed here." Rolph stepped forward and peered at the small writing. "Weary traveler," he read aloud, "you have faced the perils of our Labyrinth and survived this far. For this you deserve praise."

"Too right," Eliard huffed, but shut up when Rolph shot him a dirty look.

Rolph cleared his throat to continue. "But only by embracing our final challenge will you deserve our *blessing*."

"What does that mean?" Eliard asked.

"If you'll let me keep reading!"

"You're the one who keeps pausing dramatically."

Rolph sighed and placed his fingers to his temples. "Touch the black stone and take your leave, though venture to this depth again and this path will be closed to you. Touch our colors and receive our blessing for your continued success."

Rolph stepped back, allowing Eliard to cram himself against the plinth and read the words for himself, his mouth moving silently as he did so. Rolph looked up at Gertrude and wished he could speak with her. Touching the wellspring of power within he found that the pool hadn't only healed his wounds but also replenished his magic.

"Gertrude!" Rolph cried, the blue glow covering the dinosaur's snout. "We can leave!"

She looked from Rolph to the doorways. "HOW?"

"Touch the black stone, the one on the left."

Gertrude sidestepped to allow herself to lean over and place her small hand on the smooth onyx. To Rolph's dismay, nothing miraculous happened. No lights, no magic, nothing activated the dark stone portal beside them.

"IT IS NOT MEANT FOR ME, SUPPERLING," she whined.

"No, it's meant for *us*." Eliard's voice held a manic note that Rolph didn't like.

"What's that supposed to mean, Eliard?"

The lancer turned and held his hands up in a placating gesture. "Don't you see? We don't have to keep going. We can go home."

"Gertrude can't make it through, Eliard. We have to keep going, to get to the gate at the center of the maze. The one Gertrude can fit through."

"Maybe *you* do, but I'm getting out of here while I can."

Eliard lowered his hand to the black stone, but Rolph shoved himself between the cleric and his prize.

"You can't do this, Eliard! We've come so far," Rolph grunted, shoving at Eliard to keep him back from the button.

The larger man reached over Rolph's head, straining to touch the dark stone. "I haven't seen my family in *ages*, Rolph. My children haven't had their father for TWO YEARS. Get out of my way!"

Rolph pressed his hand against the man's face, pushing him back. "But we promised!"

The blow caught Rolph by surprise and he tumbled sideways to the floor, his ears ringing with the strength of Eliard's fist. Gertrude roared and snapped at Eliard, but the lancer held his spear menacingly toward Gertrude's face. Rolph's proximity to Eliard seemed to make Gertrude unwilling to do more than growl at the man, biting at the air above his spear.

"No," he spat. "*You* promised. Then you captured me and forced me to follow you on this harebrained adventure. Call off your pet, before I do something I'll regret."

"DO I EAT HIM NOW, TINY DINOSAUR? FOR HIS TREACHERY."

Rolph rubbed his cheek, his head spinning from the strike. He stood unsteadily, bracing himself against the wall. "No, let him go. We don't need him."

Gertrude did not seem pleased but only blew hot breath over Eliard before moving around to the larger door. Eliard, for his part, moved to stand closer to the obsidian slab, and waited.

Rolph touched the opal without hesitation. Heat flooded him like fire suffusing his body, but it was not painful. The sensation was similar to what had happened when he had killed the minotaur, only this time it was uncomfortably strong. Power seeped through his bones, and he knew his magic had been enhanced, his resilience and strength as well. When he had transitioned from Explorer to Adventurer, it had been something like this.

The mason staggered and placed his hand on the plinth to keep from falling over again. "Mother's embrace, that was a lot."

"What happened to you?" Eliard asked though his spear was still trained on Gertrude.

"You don't get to ask," Rolph growled at Eliard.

"ARE YOU ALRIGHT?" Gertrude echoed Eliard's sentiment, and Rolph smiled weakly at the dinosaur.

"I'm fine. You should try touching it, too, just in case."

Gertrude pressed her talons to the opal, but as before, nothing happened. She huffed and shook herself. "AGAIN, THIS IS NOT MEANT FOR ME."

"The gate is all we need, Gertrude. I'll get you there."

Rolph rested a hand on Gertrude's scales and the dinosaur rumbled in quiet reply. The mason pulled on the handle of the great door and to his surprise it swung open easily on near-silent hinges. He wondered what waited on the other side but threw the thought away.

"I'm keeping my promise," he said, and strode through the gate. "Even if it kills me."

Chapter Twenty-Five
MIRROR IMAGES

After passing through the Triad's gate, Rolph wasn't sure which direction he was traveling in anymore. The transition struck him as odd, just as entering the central maze had been a stark contrast to the naturally formed caverns he and Eliard had traversed on their way.

Eliard, that swine.

Leave it to the man to be exactly what he had shown himself as. A coward, through and through. Rolph wouldn't have been surprised to find that Eliard had no wife and children but clung to a lie that started back when he had met Ross and his party.

The corridors were similar to the uniform shape where he had lost Gertrude, but instead of a sandy stone these were huge blocks laid like bricks, and the floor was cobbled with large stones worn smooth over time. Sconces lined the walls here as well, torches burning brightly but the dark stone devoured much of the light. He would have expected to find something like this in a castle or battlement wall, not deep within the Labyrinth.

Everything was still sized for creatures of Gertrude's dimensions, so he felt a bit like a doll. A plaything of the Triad, traipsing through a hallway made for giants. He flexed his shoulders and neck as he walked, still reeling from the goddesses' blessing. His mind had expanded in a way as yet unclear to him, and he could tell he was stronger. Was he a Hero, now?

Rolph scoffed at himself. He would be a Hero if he got Gertrude out of there and could sit in his father's old armchair with his feet by the fire. His father... A tear formed in his eye, blurring half his vision. He blinked it away and cursed. Now was not the time to—

"Rolph!"

The cry brought Rolph back to reality in the middle of a corridor he had no memory of turning down. Gertrude walked beside him seemingly trusting that he knew the way, which he most certainly did not. Had he been so lost in thought? How many traps could he have sprung by now?

"Rolph..."

The voice came again, though weaker. He knew that tone, a familiar timbre. He turned about, scanning for doors or passageways. No rooms branched off the hall, but a four-way intersection lay ahead.

"Father?" he asked in a halting voice.

"Help me!"

The sound came from the left, as far as he could tell, and he quickened his steps. He needed to talk with Gertrude, so cast his spell as he walked. "I don't know how, but my father is down here."

Gertrude sniffed the air. "I DO NOT KNOW WHAT HE SMELLS LIKE, BUT SOME MAN-THING WALKS THE PATHS."

Turning left revealed a hallway much like the one they had just been in, but in the distant torchlight a dark shape scurried away from them. It might have been one figure, or two, it was so hard to tell.

"Wait!" Rolph yelled and the echo carried back to him as he picked up the pace further, heedless of the potential dangers.

What magic existed here? Was the triad so cruel as to bestow their blessing on him, only to steal his father away from the surface as some kind of test? He would have strong words for Alveth if he managed to find his way home again, goddesses be damned.

The shadowed figure turned right at the end of the path, as there was only one direction to go. Rolph pelted after it, his boots making sharp cracks against the stone. When he reached the turn himself, he seemed to have gained no ground and was as far from his quarry as before.

"Gertrude, I need your help!"

The dinosaur didn't ask questions but picked him up by his pack. Her teeth sank into the canvas and the chest strap pulled against him. It may have been uncomfortable, but Rolph marveled at their speed as Gertrude built into a charge. The air whipped past his face and the thing they pursued began to resolve into a cloaked humanoid. It didn't glance back at them as they approached, so he couldn't make out their face, but it was roughly the height of his father.

But then why did it run from them?

Another intersection approached, and this time their target continued straight. They had closed the gap sufficiently that Rolph had an idea. "Throw me at it!" He yelled, jostled though he was by the dinosaur's gait. With a toss of her head, Gertrude sent Rolph flying at the running creature. The pair collided and went down in a heap.

Rolph tumbled a short distance and tried to orient himself as Gertrude roared. A loud clanking noise played counterpoint to her complaint. His head whipped around at the sound and found a large iron cage had closed around the dinosaur, the equivalent of an iron portcullis fallen from each of the four directions of the intersection. She butted her head against the metal bands uselessly. Gertrude must have triggered a trap in her haste to throw him.

The body-shaped lump Rolph had collided with shifted, drawing back his attention. The dinosaur could wait a moment. He crawled closer as the cloak fell away from the man's face.

"Dad?"

He would need to throttle Alveth after all, once he was out of this, because Mason's face stared back at him. People often referred to Rolph as the spitting image of his father, albeit younger. He hadn't seen it, personally, but now that he crouched by his father, he understood why the majority of Mayfair said so.

"Rolph," Mason said.

He hadn't heard his father's voice in the years since he and his mother retired. His stomach dipped. "How did you get here? Is mom here too?"

"No, just me." Mason patted his arm and struggled to stand. Rolph hurried to help him up. "I don't know. Some kind of teleportation spell, probably?" He stretched his back, the familiar cracking along his spine filling the air.

"Why did you run from me?"

Mason gestured at the dinosaur behind Rolph. "Looks like the problem solved itself."

Gertrude struck at the cage again, a frustrated groan rumbling from her belly.

"Right." That made enough sense, Rolph figured. If he had seen his son being presumably chased by a dinosaur, he might have thought the same. "That's my friend. Speaking of…" He used this opportunity to approach the cage.

"Wait! Rolph!" Mason grasped frantically at his wrist. "You should leave it where it is!"

Rolph chuckled. "It's fine. I mean it." He gently extracted himself and turned back to Gertrude. "Let's see how we can get you out of this one," he muttered, drawing out his hammer and feeling at the solid rungs of the trap.

Gertrude's eyes narrowed at something behind him, and she bellowed a roar he hadn't heard before. The hairs on the back of his neck stood at the sound and he spun, bringing up his hammer barely in time to catch a dagger's downward slash. Mason's lips were pulled tight around a wolfish grin Rolph had never seen him wear, and an unmistakable reddish glow rimmed his irises.

He would have to apologize to Alveth. This was not his father. He pushed Not-Mason's attack off, and the man bounced lightly backwards, completely unbothered that Rolph had parried his surprise attack.

"I told you to leave it where it is," the *thing* snarled.

Gertrude's own rumbling growl vibrated through the ground beneath Rolph's feet, and Rolph used the space he had gained to set his back more central to the cage. He watched Not-Mason's footwork closely as his heart thundered in his chest. "Who are you?"

The creature pretending to be Rolph's father laughed in Mason's voice, but it was a distortion of the merriment Mason's laughter normally carried. "What do you mean, Rolph? I *am* your father."

"You're nothing like him." Rolph eyed the ground beneath his father's doppelganger's feet. If he moved quickly, he might be able to summon some vines to root him in place. He just had to move carefully.

Not-Mason gave Rolph a slight pout. "I thought I did pretty good." He rubbed the edge of his jaw. "Dear old dad wasn't an easy maneuver, after all. Memories from a distance are...finicky."

He moved more quickly than Rolph's eyes could follow, launching himself across the space, dagger held low. The mason tried to call on the spell he had discovered during their last fight and struggled to push magic into the ground through his legs and feet. Vines erupted between them, reaching greedily for his opponent.

He couldn't pinpoint specifically where the doppelganger's ankles might be, but he figured if he covered enough surface area, it might do the job.

While the vines didn't catch the doppelganger's feet, it forced him to sidestep the patch, allowing Rolph enough time to levy a defense. He brought his hammer up to push the dagger away and leveraged his foot between them—shoving as hard as he could manage. The doppelganger stumbled backwards, but dipped and twisted, returning another blow, forcing Rolph to step backwards with each swipe and thrust.

Gertrude let out a desperate roar from behind them and tried butting her way through the bars, smashing her head against it again and again. If Rolph had any shred of attention to spare, he would have been concerned that she would hurt herself before making any progress getting out.

"Pretty little thing you have there," the doppelganger nodded to the hammer as Rolph caught another glancing blow off the end of it. Rolph's arms shook with the effort of fending off his attacker and sweat trickled down the back of his neck. He couldn't pause to fully consider how much danger he was in; he couldn't allow himself to freeze up. Not if he wanted to get out of this alive—not if he wanted to get Gertrude out alive.

"You like it?" Rolph taunted back, searching for an opening. "My *father* gave it to *me*," on the last syllable, he shoved *hard* against his opponent and threw his magic into the thrust. Vines erupted from the ground and climbed the doppelganger's legs, pulling him away from Rolph's grasp and rooting him to the floor.

Gertrude roared an eager affirmative. Were Rolph able to understand her, he expected she was telling him to finish the creature off. Instead, the figure's face shifted, and Rolph couldn't help but stare as it contorted into a visage that horrified him.

The mirror image of his own features.

Chapter Twenty-Six
A Bit of "Self" Loathing

Rolph stumbled backwards in surprise.

"Useless," Rolph's own voice said to him. "What are you even trying to do, here? You're way out of your depth."

Rolph, the real one, didn't know much about doppelgangers. The creature had mentioned something about memories from a distance, but now that they were face-to-face it stared into his eyes like it knew his soul. His conjured vines held the monster's dagger immobile, but muscles that appeared stronger than the ones they mimicked strained against their bonds.

"I'm just trying to get home," Rolph panted. He sucked in air, trying to catch his breath after the flurry of attacks from his erstwhile twin.

"You're going to die here, just like the rest of them. No one survives an encounter with my master."

Master? This was the first time Rolph had heard reference to the foe at the center of the maze. He thought quickly, wondering if there was a way to turn the encounter to his advantage. "If that's so, let me go then. If your master is sure to kill me, what harm would there be in letting me walk into the jaws of the lion?"

His mirror twin laughed in contempt and Rolph hoped he never sounded like that. "We all have our purpose. Well, not you perhaps. I couldn't find a single reason to keep living in that head of yours."

"Rude," Rolph complained. This was not going the way he had hoped. "What's *your* reason for being here?"

"I was created for the trials, like any creature here. But more specifically, I'm here to distract, and ultimately kill you."

"Simple enough, I suppose." Rolph sniffed the air and the scent of something burning tickled his nose.

Gertrude roared plaintively and Rolph reached for his magic so he could understand whatever she was trying to tell him. Unfortunately, he came up empty, his efforts to ensnare the doppelganger had burned through the last of his reserves. He examined the scene in front of him, searching for what was out of place. The vines still held his enemy, who held a glowing red dagger, except...its weapon had been plain steel before.

"Well, that's no good," he whined and leaped forward to swing his hammer at the doppelganger's wrist. As if in slow motion the cherry-red blade sizzled through the remainder of the vine, allowing its hand to drop a hair's width before Rolph's strike would have hit true. Instead, in a lightning-quick maneuver, his opponent flipped the dagger into a reverse grip and leaned the blade against Rolph's forearm, pressing down.

Rolph cried out in pain and dropped his sole weapon. In three quick slashes, the doppelganger freed its remaining limbs from their verdant bonds and kicked Rolph's hammer skittering across the corridor.

"You won't be needing that anymore. Wouldn't want to hurt *yourself* now, would you?" It gave him a wink and a leering smile.

Rolph backed away as cautiously as he could. Just because he and Gertrude had sprung this creature's trap didn't mean there wasn't another waiting for him.

Traps.

Rolph reached around and unshouldered Fern's staff. The overcomplicated walking stick had been his constant companion, testing their path for hidden dangers. Now it was the closest thing to a weapon he had left to hand.

"See," Rolph replied. "If you think I like myself enough to not hurt a copy of me, you need to dig a little deeper."

He hefted the would-be cudgel and swung it at his opponent, who sidestepped nimbly now that he wasn't entangled. The doppelganger lunged again, trying to get inside Rolph's reach. The mason slapped the attack aside with his staff, throwing orange sparks at the contact. The dagger being enchanted was a concern, but he hoped the staff's properties at least imbued it with a bit of magical resilience.

"You're using Fandring's staff as a club? You should lay down and let me end your suffering, man-child."

Rolph bristled at the talk, even though he accepted it was meant to goad him. He didn't know the staff had a name, nor any use of it, because the only wizard present on this level had been squashed to a pulp by the dinosaur imprisoned behind him. He pressed his attack, holding it like a quarterstaff, striking to the right and left with as much power and speed as he could muster.

With each hit, his evil twin twitched its dagger side to side, blocking each swing. Colorful sprays of light followed each, like a hammer on hot iron. Rolph's face and neck boiled with rage. "I'm. Not. Even. Supposed. To be. *Here!*"

The last blow slipped under the dagger's guard and took his foe in the chest, driving the breath from its lungs with a sharp exhalation. It wasn't enough, it seemed. Even though the thing stepped back, it wasn't in retreat, but into another guard posture. It held its blade horizontally in front to ward off more attacks.

"I see the cub has teeth. It really is too bad you'll never see your father again. He might finally be *proud of you* for something."

Rolph took the end of the staff in two hands, raised it high above his head, and brought it down against the doppelganger with all the force his magically enhanced strength gave him. The other "man" raised his dagger to parry, but the glint of humor in the creature's eyes vanished when the two weapons collided and the staff *exploded*.

Rolph flew backward and slammed into the metal lattice of Gertrude's cage. His vision swam and faded to white. For an indeterminate amount of time, Rolph was blind to the world around him. His eyes overflowed with tears, his chest ached like he had been headbutted by the village bull, and his ears rang. Gertrude cried out, but her voice was muffled and distant. Rolph's equilibrium failed, and he fell onto his side. The T-Rex's face peered sideways at him as his eyes closed, and consciousness fled.

When Rolph awoke, it was to a massive wet tongue running across his face. He pushed the disgusting muscle away with a miserable groan. His blurry eyesight notwithstanding, Rolph couldn't mistake the fact that Gertrude had freed herself from her iron prison. He rubbed liberally at his face and eventually the binocular vision he had always taken for granted returned.

"I must have been out cold," Rolph mused, taking in the scene. The side of the portcullis-like cage had burst outward. The riveted bands had popped and torn, and clearly Gertrude had forced her bulk through the opening until it was large enough to accommodate her.

Rolph tried to cast his communication spell, but the attempt fizzled as it had when he fought the doppelganger.

Crone's beard, what happened to the doppelganger?

Rolph shook a bit more of the fuzziness from his head and forced himself to his feet. His balance was still compromised, but he steadied himself against a convenient dinosaur leg as he peered about for his foe. An unfamiliar creature, tall, gray, and sickly, lay sprawled some twenty feet down the hall from where he had ended up. It didn't move, but from that distance Rolph couldn't tell if it was still breathing.

He gave himself a once-over, patting his torso down to his extremities. Everything hurt. At least one of his ribs might be fractured given the pain when he breathed, but nothing else appeared to be broken. Fern's staff, which Not-Rolph had identified as some kind of named artifact, lay near his resting place.

Half of it, anyway.

The young druid stooped to pick it up, nearly keeling over in the process. He took a moment to recover from the difficulty of his miniscule effort, making noises that would have put a grin on his father's face. Rolph then made his way to the side of the corridor and retrieved his hammer. The staff hadn't been his first choice, and now that it was broken it was even further down his list of preferred weapons. When Rolph had wielded it like a long club, swinging with all his might from one end, he hadn't expected the item to, well, explode. It was magical—or had been, and magic items were known for their uncommon resilience. Sure, they could break, but it usually took more than one parry from an albeit enchanted dagger to destroy them.

His fingers slid over the wood and his thumbnail caught on a flaw where it had snapped, splintered and rough. No, this was a nick, a scored line of some kind. It was almost as if something powerful had scratched at it with a claw...

Gertrude must have damaged it when she crushed Fern to death, he surmised. *Which inadvertently saved my life. Again.*

Gertrude followed him with her gaze but padded behind him when he approached the spindly thing on the ground. Its true form was taller than either of the figures it had been impersonating, wearing a nondescript outfit of heavy linen. It seemed whatever magic it possessed allowed it to transform not only its body, but clothing as well. That, or it was a separate talent. From the blood seeping out of the creature's nose, and the missing half of its chest laying another five feet away from it, Rolph would never get the chance to ask.

"Probably would have said something insulting, anyway. Like how I was too stupid to know the difference between talents and spells," Rolph complained, though Gertrude only snuffed in reply.

Rolph spied the magical dagger laying off to the side and mentally marked it for retrieval. The only other gear the fallen doppelganger had was a belt pouch. It contained a few vials, but two were smashed into fragments leaving only the stoppers intact. The liquid staining the leather wouldn't be any use to him. The one remaining bottle was a deep, ruby red.

"Maiden's tears!" Rolph cried, pulling the cork with his teeth and draining the contents in one mighty swallow. The relief spread through his wounded and weary body instantly, and he sighed almost indecently. Gertrude only snorted.

"You were out of commission for this fight, and I needed it more than you did." Rolph peered through Gertrude's legs at the remainder of the cage, longing for a trip back to the healing spring in Trike's stable. There was no likely way to get there, unless he wanted to convince Gertrude to peel the rest of the trap like a metal onion.

Small gashes and scrapes covered the dinosaur's face and shoulders where she had forced herself through. Rolph grimaced, even considering asking her to injure herself further for the sake of a hot soak.

With a renewed spring in his step, Rolph did a final pass of the area to scoop up the dagger and check for anything he had missed.

"C'mon. Let's put some distance between us and this place before another servant of *the master* shows up to insult my life choices."

Chapter Twenty-Seven
PROMISES, PROMISES

The pair traveled for what seemed like the rest of the "day" before stopping for rest. Rolph still couldn't wrap his head around the change in architecture, though given there were three goddesses in the Triad, he tried to accept it all as simply another phase. The dark, fitted stone of these new corridors was so different from the earlier sandy, roughly chiseled hallways.

Rolph considered it as they walked, turning the broken pieces of Fandring's staff over in his hands. The unfinished, but bright passages before had been the Maiden's. These were the Mother's, strong and serviceable. What would be next? Rotting wood and cobwebs for the Crone?

They walked on until they found an offshoot of the corridors which might have served as a larder or storeroom if this were a keep. More round than square, it sat in the elbow of an L turn in their path. Without Eliard to conjure rations for delver stew, Rolph tucked into a cold meal of mushroom jerky and once again thanked the Shulzuh for their hospitality. Even without the ability to speak, Gertrude insisted on taking watch by planting herself firmly in the doorway, which had no door to speak of until she lay across it.

He awoke in the morning with a heavy heart. Another serving of his dwindling supplies did nothing to assuage the hollow feeling in his gut. Eliard had abandoned them, and the specter of his father had tried to kill him. Rolph knew it wasn't Mason, but the hope that had bloomed in his heart at seeing the man left a void when it turned out to be a trap.

He was physically exhausted, but moreover the emotional toll of the past two days had drained him. While the promise made to Gertrude was important to him, Rolph suddenly longed for home. He missed the relatively calm days he had spent in the stonemason shop. There, even as unskilled and stressed as he was about making ends meet, he wasn't in mortal danger at any given moment. Nor was he forced to face a monster wearing a loved one's face. The Labyrinth was a sick and twisted "blessing" from the Triad.

He chewed on a tasteless mushroom, reminiscing about a time when he only made friends with the mice and the sad drunkards in the tavern. Gertrude was slow to rise that morning, but after the day they'd had before, he was content to let her sleep. He wasn't sure where they would go from there. Rolph had to pick a direction and start, or he might lie there with Gertrude until they rotted away.

"*Rolph,*" an urgent whisper from beyond the archway called.

Rolph's blood went cold. The voice was unmistakable. He stood from where he sat gnawing on a particularly chewy piece of fungus. "Eliard?"

The cleric stepped into the light cast by the single torch burning in the annex they had slept in. "I'm sorry I left." His voice echoed against the stone walls as he walked. Gertrude raised her head from where she slept and sniffed.

Rolph was not ashamed to admit it, tears welled in his eyes, and he wiped them away with the back of his hand. "Why did you come back?"

"It was a mistake. I shouldn't have let you go on alone." Eliard opened his arms as if offering Rolph a hug.

Rolph's mouth twisted with a wry smile. He stepped forward into the other man's embrace. "I'm glad you came back." A gurgling sound immediately followed, as the dagger he had rescued from the other doppelganger found its mark in an upward thrust through Eliard's abdomen.

"Rolph?!" Eliard's eyes went wide, but his shape began to transform.

"Eliard would never have hugged me, you overconfident copy." Rolph twisted the knife for good measure and was rewarded with a spray of blood from the thing's chest. He wasn't sure yet how to activate the magical properties of the weapon, so this would have to do. "Your master is next."

Rolph stepped back, letting the body of another doppelganger fall to the floor. He retrieved two additional healing potions from this one's pouch, which hadn't suffered any damage from this much less eventful encounter.

"It's just you and me, now." He looked at Gertrude, then motioned to the body on the floor. She needed no further encouragement and snapped it up, throwing the corpse into the air before catching it in her wide mouth.

The young mason returned to his squat to finish his meager breakfast. As Gertrude finished her own meal, the crunching of bones didn't bother him for once.

Their journey continued in a similar, if less dramatic fashion. Rolph found another stick to replace Fern's staff for trap-finding purposes, augmented with his detection spell. The power he had received from the Triad, compensating him for risking his life in this next part of the Labyrinth, helped set their pace. With Gertrude's power, and Rolph's growing skill, they made their way through uncounted twists and turns.

Rolph continued marking his path, though he began using the heat of the flame-dagger once he found the correct sigil to press on its hilt. It wouldn't do to get turned around when they were as close as he felt to their goal, plus it was helpful when he needed to make a fire from whatever material he could scrounge. No dinosaur-sized pit traps caught Gertrude, nor did bands of miscreants threaten to chase them back down into the tunnels. To the benefit of Rolph's sanity, they didn't encounter any more doppelgangers.

What monsters they found, they fought. Rolph experienced the same tingling sensation indicating his reward from the Triad, but he feared no amount of grinding himself against the mortar of the maze would make a difference. He was done and wanted to go home. There was little left to do besides test himself against this "master" he had been threatened with. Nonetheless, he threw himself into their small skirmishes with a fatalism that added confidence to his hammer swings.

The T-Rex was well-fed if nothing else.

It took longer than Rolph wanted, and they backtracked on his markings multiple times, but after another two days of painstaking travel, he found himself staring at another set of massive doors. They were tall black things, carved in bas relief. He picked out animals from within the Labyrinth, depicted in stunning detail on the ebony wood. Among the menagerie sat a likeness of the Crone. Normally depicted with silver hair, the lack of color in this work was striking. The ravages of time, wrinkles and all, stared back at him.

At least his hunch about the composition of the Labyrinth had been right. He lifted his hand to the huge iron ring hanging on one side but as he touched the metal, the door swung silently open.

Rolph turned to the dinosaur, who curved her neck to peer into the doorway, then glanced down at him. He rested his palm on her leg.

"We're going home, Gertrude. I promise."

Chapter Twenty-Eight
THIS IS NOT WHAT I EXPECTED

A GROTTO, NOT DISSIMILAR to Trike's stable, greeted Rolph on the other side of the door. Though where the other dinosaur's lair had been utilitarian and ascetic, this was a verdant opulence Rolph wouldn't have expected to find in the depths.

It wasn't that there were trees and grass, no, but analogs to them abounded. Moss, plush like the bed he had slept on in Shulzuh, covered the majority of the floor. The path in front of him was stone, the same as the hallways they had just been through, but the edges were covered in living landscape.

He stood in quiet awe and in the silence the trickle of a stream caught his ear. He cast his gaze about and caught a glimpse of a small rivulet running through the subterranean garden. A sweet perfume in the air tickled his nostrils and he coughed slightly at the aroma. Gertrude huffed similarly, making a reptilian equivalent.

Instead of trees, giant mushrooms dotted the room. It was larger than even the chamber containing the cistern had been. The ceilings were higher, as well. Torches were fewer and farther between, intermixed with some of the glowing fungus from the roughest parts of this level. All in all, it mimicked a dimly lit evening in a forest glade, except it was ninety-five levels below the ground and nothing was as it should have been.

"What brings you here, young one?"

Rolph jumped. His fingers darted to the hammer at his belt in automatic response to the grizzled and high-pitched voice.

Sitting among the moss, with a staff made from a curled tree root resting next to him, was a diminutive kobold. Rolph had never seen one before, and despite its slightly monstrous appearance, it addressed him in perfect Common. After his experience with D'zrt, Rolph was less surprised than he could have been. The kobold had a characteristically long and narrow face, punctuated by scaly outcroppings across the crown of his head. The most unusual part of his appearance had less to do with his physical attributes, and more to do with the fact that he wore spectacles and loose-fitting clothing.

Rolph hesitated and let his hammer fall back to his side. "Sorry, I didn't see you," he said. The kobold didn't reply, only looked up at him with those beady eyes. Rolph scanned the newfound scenery. "Where is here? And who are you?"

The kobold appraised him, as though he wasn't certain if he wanted to divulge the information to Rolph. "I don't suppose you made it to the center of this maze without knowing what you were getting into."

Rolph's nerves bristled. It wasn't the kobold's words, but the way he said them that put the mason on edge. "You might be surprised," he replied, keeping his tone even. "I didn't actually make it here in the usual way."

"What is the usual way?" The kobold asked.

Rolph found himself shrugging, though a tiny voice in the back of his head wondered why he was being so conversational. There was something about this place, a peace smoothed the ruffled edges of his nerves. "You know, you get some people together, hack and slash your way down. You make plans." He splayed his fingers in demonstration, like laying a map out on a table. "I didn't have the luxury."

"Interesting. What brought you down here?"

Rolph felt the day wear on him. The kobold seemed pleasant enough, and he hadn't had much of a chance for casual conversation that wasn't talking to Gertrude (mostly himself) or Eliard. "May I sit?" The kobold nodded and gestured to a patch of grass opposite him, and Rolph sat. A pleasant scent wafted to his nose, and he inhaled deeply, settling into the comfortable moss. Gertrude grumbled, but he ignored her. "That's the thing, I'm not supposed to be here," the mason explained. "A freak accident, really. Fell through my basement."

The kobold nodded sagely. "Sometimes we are brought places we never would have otherwise been."

Rolph shrugged. "I don't really believe in fate, but I *am* glad I'm here. Sort of."

Gertrude rumbled deep in her throat again, and from the corner of his eye, he caught her crouching, as though preparing to pounce. "Hey! We don't need that. We're just chatting." Gertrude whined but relaxed a little. "Sorry, I don't know what's got into her," he said politely, but the kobold simply shook his head.

"It's no bother." He slowly drew himself up, standing about as tall as Rolph's collarbone, were he to stand himself. "Fate is an interesting thing," the kobold mused. "Considering your surprising entrance."

"Is it? Surprising?"

"Isn't that what you just told me? I'm only being conversational. Unless you're here to kill me, that is."

"Certainly not." Rolph laughed and it turned into an expansive yawn. His head swam when his jaw snapped shut. It hadn't been too long since he'd slept, but he could go for a lie-down. The kobold was a pleasant surprise, all things considered. Maybe whatever the Triad had in store for him wasn't a fight to the death, after all. "I'm not much of a warrior. Found out I'm a druid, of all things."

"Really? Underestimated people, druids." The kobold nodded sagely. "Natural magic is powerful."

Rolph didn't know this kobold from a hole in the ground, but part of his mind rebelled at him for chatting away like he was drunk on buch back in Shulzuh. "Who are you, anyway? And why are *you* here?" He was proud of himself for putting the smaller creature on the spot. Something rustled near his leg and startled him, but the kobold raised a calming hand.

"Don't worry about them." Its voice droned on and lulled him back to rest. "My name is Karvalak, and this is my grotto. It's a place for weary delvers to rest before the final trial."

"That's very kind of you." The mason nodded and his eyelids drooped. They remained closed for half a heartbeat before he forced them open again. The moss *was* comfortable, and he could use another nap if the last encounter was ahead.

Rolph checked on his dinosaur companion. Gertrude hadn't laid down but crouched near to the ground, her own eyes fighting against the pull of sleep. She seemed decidedly uncomfortable, though, compared to his own calm. Her large feet shifted nervously under her, and she snapped weakly at the air.

"It's so…relaxing…here…" Rolph said with a mouth thick with impending sleep. He let his eyes close, leaning back into the dense moss.

The kobold nodded. "Yes. That's the poison. It makes it much easier for the larvae to eat you."

Yes, that makes sense, he thought dreamily. The greenery shifted beneath him and chittering, much like a sound he had heard elsewhere in the Labyrinth, reached his ears. Then Rolph's eye snapped open, though they did try to close immediately again. The surge of adrenaline through his system fought against his lethargy and roused him from his state of impending unconsciousness. He sat up with a jolt. "The *what?*"

Rolph reached blindly for his magic and cast the first spell he could think of in his addled state. An enormous green, glowing circle surrounded him stretching at least one hundred feet in every direction. Karvalak sat grinning amidst the results of his spell.

The entire room was a trap.

Chapter Twenty-Nine

GOOD, BAD, I'M THE GUY WITH THE DINOSAUR

Rolph's head still spun as he tried to understand what was happening. Karvalak said nothing, only staring at Rolph with a wide-toothed smile.

His brain was slow to catch up, but he finally grasped what Karvalak had said. *Poison!*

Rolph's next move was a gamble, betting against his lack of delving knowledge. He fumbled at his pouch until he came away with one of the two healing potions recovered from the doppelgangers. Rolph had no idea what the limit of the magical draughts were, or whether they would cure his affliction, but he was too far gone to consider other options.

He pulled the cork with his teeth and took a swallow. The lethargy faded from his limbs and his thoughts sharpened again. Rolph would have whooped for joy if Gertrude hadn't taken that moment to stumble to the side, about to pitch over. He scrambled to his feet and ran to her. Casting his communication spell, the blue glow taking its usual perch on the carnivore's snout, he shouted.

"Open wide!"

Thankfully, she did just that, and Rolph pitched the remainder of the potion straight down her gullet. Whether the poison had affected her less, or the enchantment ignored things like body mass, Gertrude's pupils widened and she clambered to her feet. She snapped at Karvalak, but the kobold's nimbleness belied his kindly-old-sage appearance and he leapt clear of her jaws before they closed around him.

The small monster whirled, bringing his staff around to point at Rolph. He muttered something and the end of it glowed a sickly red. The mason barely jumped out of the way as a malevolent bolt screamed toward him.

A magic user, too? Rolph complained inwardly.

He took a bad tumble avoiding a second bolt, landing heavily on his shoulder with an unpleasant crunch. Rolph rolled over one of the squirming lumps in the moss and a pair of razor-sharp pincers tore through the lush ground cover. The disgusting form of a cave crawler nymph wriggled into the open air.

He scanned the area and an oddity in the geometry caught his eye. The glowing trap, visible only to Rolph, hadn't centered itself on the kobold. No, if he did some mental measurements the center was twenty feet away where there appeared to be an extremely large, hollow, trunk of a tree.

The problem with that observation was there had been no other trees in the room. Yes, subterranean equivalents dotted the landscape, mosses and large ferns that thrived on damp and neglect, but the trunk was distinctly out of place. If that wasn't indicator enough, the sickly-sweet smell he had noticed earlier became stronger when he pointed his nose in that direction.

Rolph took a desperate chance. He didn't want to throw away one of his only real weapons, but he still wasn't much of a fighter beyond swinging his hammer. As he rounded Gertrude's large body he drew the flame dagger. He used the dinosaur's bulk to grant himself some cover, though he immediately worried she would become the target of Karvalak's spells. Given how large she was even he could hit the side of a barn, so Rolph decided it was mostly unavoidable.

He pressed the sigil to ignite the blade, drew his arm back, and threw with all his might toward the tree trunk. Rolph's aim was true, and luck was with him as the steel sank to the hilt. The enchanted steel passed much deeper than he expected, and a hideous screech erupted from his target. The shape and color of the trunk wavered and changed, resolving into a disgusting, gray, fleshy mass. It had large mandibles which clacked menacingly but only swayed back and forth. The multiple legs along its sides alternately reached for nothing and tried to grasp at the dagger piercing its side.

The nymphs crawling through the undergrowth let out high keening calls. Rolph didn't know this monster, but he deduced it must have been a queen of some type. The larvae under the moss were its children, and he had almost fallen *asleep* on them. He shuddered then raised his voice.

"GERTRUDE! KILL THAT THING!"

Rolph didn't have to tell her twice. Gertrude roared, nearly deafening him. She clearly had *not* liked that Karvalak, and his pet monstrosity had tried to kill them. The dinosaur stooped as if she was going to bite the creature in half but seemed to think twice as the pungent aroma hit her nostrils. She growled, spun, and struck the thing with the meaty part of her tail. Rolph anticipated the creature sailing to a far wall, but instead it *disintegrated*.

Pink guts, gray flesh, and larval jelly sprayed everywhere as the impact atomized the cave crawler queen. Rolph gorge rose as he was hit with ichor and blood but he choked it back, turning to Karvalak who stared at him in horror.

"So—" Rolph tried to say but couldn't stop himself from dry heaving instead. He held up a hand to forestall the Kobold from interrupting. "Was that the test?"

Karvalak chuckled and straightened his posture, his back popped loudly as he lengthened his spine and stood nearly to Rolph's height. It wasn't as tall as it sounded but Rolph wasn't a tall man, so it struck him as impressive, nonetheless.

"No, human. That was merely to weed out the less intelligent challengers." He eyed Gertude, who was trying to shake the queen's remains off her scales. They locked gazes and the dinosaur lunged toward him. Karvalak raised his staff and an emerald glow erupted from it, a beam streaking toward Gertrude.

"Stop!" Rolph screamed and held his palm out to Gertrude. He reached for his magic again, feeling something new. He didn't understand the whole of it but *pushed* the same way he had when he had detected a trap for the first time. A white light burst from his outstretched hand and reached Gertrude's muzzle before the other magic user's. It spread over her entire body like she had bathed in a crystalline pool.

Karvalak's spell bounced harmlessly off the shell, and he stood wide-eyed. "You are more powerful than I gave you credit for, little druid. You resisted my poison, killed my minion, and denied me your dinosaur."

"I'll do more than that," Rolph blustered.

Karvalak gave him a manic grin. "Mayhap. But you won't deny me *mine*."

"Your what?" Rolph swallowed heavily.

A roar sounded from the far side of the room where Rolph hadn't ventured. It lay partially in shadow, and to Rolph's dismay it had clearly hidden something from their initial inspection. Massive thumps pulsed through the floor, and the mason was suddenly reminded of his time tied to a stake at the other end of this level.

"No…" Rolph said, almost too softly to hear.

Much like a moment so many days prior, the first thing to become visible out of the darkness was a snout. Rows of sharp teeth the size of Rolph's torso reflected the dim light, and eye-shine glinted brightly as the massive predator's head swung this way and that. Rolph couldn't believe it, but the beast *sauntered* lazily into view. It could have passed for an older sibling of Gertrude's, and it stood a half-head taller than *his* dinosaur.

It yawned in a surprisingly cat-like gesture, inhaled a great breath, and then bellowed a challenge. Rolph glanced nervously at Gertrude, who rolled her eyes. The gigantic monster distracted both of them as Karvalak ran to greet it. The diminutive spellcaster emitted a brief golden burst and levitated high enough to reach the creature's back where a saddle waited for him. Rolph hadn't taken in the minute details and had missed a pattern of leather straps ornamenting its torso securing the seat. Karvalak waited mid-air as the monster turned to allow him to descend and secure himself.

"What in the name of the Triad is going on?" Rolph asked aloud.

"SHE IS ANOTHER COUSIN, SUPPERLING," Gertrude whined.

"You know her?"

"NO, BUT I AM AWARE OF HER KIND, THE GIANTS." Gertrude blew a disdainful snort. "SHE IS THE WORST."

Rolph took in the new dinosaur and tried to pinpoint differences between the two. The "giant," besides being taller, had a larger mass than Gertrude. Her tail was also slimmer, and the way she moved inclined Rolph to believe she would be nimbler on her feet than Gertrude.

Karvalak cackled brightly from his high seat. "If you yield now, I will grant you a merciful death!"

Rolph sighed. Karvalak was also, apparently, going to be the worst. If there was one thing the mason was mightily sick of during his entire experience below the earth, it was powerful beings threatening him in dramatic ways. He readied his hammer and considered whether any of his magic could be brought to bear. "No, thank you. I've got bills waiting for me at home. Very important, you see."

His magic must have translated his words in an appropriate way as Gertrude hissed a lizard-like chuckle at the joke. Rolph grinned as well, considering how far he had come from cowering behind a stalagmite to quipping at mortal enemies. Despite his levity, the situation was dire. He reckoned it didn't matter at this point. It was much better to die with a joke on his tongue than with soiled pants.

Their tactic for splitting the attention of the triceratops and rider wouldn't work here. For one, they no longer had Eliard and his magic. None of Rolph's spells seemed optimal for combat, and even his thorny shield wouldn't deter the giant if she was as agile as he feared. Second, splitting up wouldn't help the pair. Karvalak was just as likely to ignore Rolph in favor of eliminating the real threat in the room and save squashing him for last.

"What do we do, Gertrude?"

"WE ARE SO CLOSE, TINY DINOSAUR. WE FIGHT."

Rolph nodded and tightened his grip on his hammer. "I did promise, didn't I?"

In a hero's journey from the stories of his youth, Rolph could have imagined charging at the gigantic monster in front of them. His pragmatic nature told him, however, that would have been stupid. Instead, they held their ground together. "Wait for the charge and try to get out of the way?" Gertrude nodded without taking her eyes off the enemy.

The Giganotosaurus, for Rolph could think of her as nothing else, scraped her feet against the ground. She tore up swathes of moss and sent cave-crawler nymphs flying before charging the two of them. Rolph waited until the rider and his massive steed got closer, then tried to recreate the spell from the last battle. He dredged it up from somewhere in his core, focusing, and concentrated on a spot ten feet in front of them. A root-shield covered in thorny protrusions sprang into existence. Rolph tensed, waiting to find out if his trap would work.

Karvalak whooped with glee, and the giant gracefully side-stepped the oversized caltrop, barely breaking her stride. Gertude set her back foot and grunted as the larger dinosaur slammed into her. The mass difference between the two was obvious, and Gertrude slid backward, losing ground to her larger opponent. She twisted her neck and tried to bite Karvalak from his perch on the other dinosaur's back.

Gertrude's jaws snapped shut over empty air, feet away from her intended target. Karvalak's mount turned her own massive teeth on Gertrude's exposed neck and sank them deeply into her flesh. Gertrude screamed in rage and thrashed against the bite, freeing herself but leaving a large flap of scaly skin in her opponent's mouth. The T-Rex placed the bony part of her skull against the monster's neck and gave a mighty shove, knocking it slightly off balance.

Through all this, Rolph fought his own instincts to rush in. He could do little against a creature of that size, and there was no fancy saddle for him to ride Gertrude into their final battle. It was more likely he would get trampled underfoot than be helpful. Instead, he visually searched the room for anything useful. The only things he found were more nymphs crawling through the undergrowth, trying to flee from the battle waging above them.

Rolph had what was perhaps the worst idea he'd had so far and said a quick prayer. "Maiden forgive me, Mother guide my hand, and Crone bless this idiotic plan…"

As Gertrude circled the larger beast, and the pair sized each other up for the next encounter, Rolph scanned the ground. He found a shape moving *away* from him, which was what he wanted. He grimaced and shoved his hands into the deep moss and grasped at the slimy body of a nymph. It writhed and wriggled but continued trying to move in the opposite direction. It didn't bring its mandibles around to bite at Rolph, yet anyway.

He heaved and drew the squealing monstrosity above the ground, swinging it around to keep the small, razor-sharp jaws away from him. He continued his circular arc until he was pointed in roughly the right direction and released the creature with a mighty throw into the air, sailing directly toward Karvalak.

This first strike didn't hit the mark. It passed over the kobold's shoulder, close enough to distract him but not enough to be a true threat. That being said, Rolph's smile broadened in triumph for having gotten even that far. Perhaps when all this was said and done, he'd enter next year's hammer-toss during the Mayfair summer games. Rolph repeated his attack, grabbing yet another fleeing nymph. This time he suffered small lacerations before he was able to send it flying toward his intended target, but the nymph struck the saddle and skittered over the top of it before falling to the floor.

This might work, Rolph thought. Unfortunately, that was also the moment when everything went wrong.

Chapter Thirty
THE WINDS OF CHANGE

Karvalak turned his attention on the young mason throwing small monsters in his direction. His staff began to glow a familiar, sickly crimson and Rolph knew bolts of magic were in his future. Rolph dove as Karvalak fired at him, hitting the moss instead. He landed heavily with a disgusting squish and was immediately set upon by other young cave-crawlers.

They swarmed over him, some biting with their sharp mandibles, others simply using his body as a bridge to move farther away. He fought to regain his feet, kicking the things off and earning more lacerations in the process. Eventually he stood and jumped away only to be struck in the chest by a red lance of magic. It bowled him over, sending him sprawling onto a segment of the stone pathway this time.

The only positive was it was bereft of nymphs, and he groaned in pain as he reoriented himself. Gertrude fought valiantly, trading attacks with her opponent. The T-Rex even spun to lash out with her tail, sending the other dinosaur sliding. Unfortunately, she received another bite for her trouble. The larger raptor latched onto the tip of her tail and pulled, yanking her feet out from under her so she fell to the ground, sending up a spray of ichor from the nymphs she crushed.

Gertrude groaned and rolled, lashing out at the gigantic dinosaur with her clawed feet. She had suffered multiple wounds at this point. Her neck, the first place she had been struck, seeped blood through the skin. He couldn't tell if she had lost the tip of her tail, or if it was simply broken. For each rake of claws she gave as she tried to stand, she received one in kind as the swifter of the two darted in to tag Gertrude with her own talons.

The giant must have felt like she had the upper hand, as she freely traded blow for blow. Rolph watched as a helpless sickness spread in his stomach. Karvalak must have given him up for dead or defeated as he lay there, for he turned his attention to Gertrude. The kobold raised his arms, and the staff took on a malevolent green hue that reflected in Gertrude's eyes. The T-Rex's movements slowed, she was clearly tiring and losing blood.

I have to do something, Rolph thought. He was injured himself, but not to the same degree. He fished the final healing potion from his pouch and climbed to his feet again. Rolph had made it three steps across the moss when Karvalak shot an emerald beam from his staff, straight into Gertrude's chest. She roared and it turned into a shrill keening as the light burned into her. Her scales smoked and blistered, like the kobold had poured acid onto her. At the same time his mount dove in and struck with its teeth. The monster wrapped her jaws around Gertrude's throat with a sickening crunch.

Rolph screamed in wordless rage and threw the potion at Gertrude. Something broke inside him as her strange wail continued. He didn't watch the glass bottle, knowing his aim was true enough to hit something Gertrude's size. No, his focus had turned inward. Something built within his chest; a feeling he didn't recognize.

The roar tore from his lips before the rest of his body bent against itself. More than a painful experience, it was a wildly disorienting one. Bones snapped and bent, the itchy sensation of scales emerging from his skin. He fell to his hands and knees and watched in bewilderment as his fingers elongated into sharp talons, and his vision sharpened. The crawling of the nymphs was painfully audible, and his brain buzzed with the onslaught of the new sensory information.

Once his body stopped stretching, Rolph's skin ached and was excruciatingly sensitive, like he had sloughed a sunburn. He glanced down at his taloned hands and marveled. They were short, lizard-like arms. He groaned, and it came out as a weak rumble, similar to Gertrude's.

I'm a dinosaur! he thought, followed immediately by *Gertrude!* He whipped his head back to her. The Giganotosaurus towered over the smaller dinosaur, left where she had dropped her.

He moved slowly at first, but his hesitant steps quickly grew into massive strides steady on splayed feet. His limbs carried him across the space faster than he had ever run, but he barely noticed. Rolph reached deep into himself, searching for one more trick, another piece of magic he could leverage to save his friend. Something inside him responded, burning through his limbs and as he ran, he *grew*.

His vantage point, already higher than his normally short stature, grew taller. Rolph wasn't eye-to-eye with the giant, nor would he have reached Gertrude's chin, but whatever he had done to himself placed him level with the larger dinosaur's arm. He launched himself at the monster, sinking his teeth into the soft area beneath her arm, where it met her chest.

The dinosaur screamed and wriggled, trying to throw him off of her. He dug in tighter, punching his talons into her scaly hide to anchor himself. Warm blood splashed over his tongue, and he fought between revulsion and exultation, a new primal part of his brain responding to the unfamiliar flavor. Despite his efforts to hold on, the Giganotosaurus heaved and tossed Rolph backward, but not without sending a small portion of its flesh with him.

Rolph shook his head, spitting out the gobbets of meat that clung to his teeth. He threw his head back and screamed. When he trained his gaze on his enemy again, he caught an incredulous T-Rex staring at him from the ground. Her wounds had partially closed, but one potion wasn't going to bring her back to full strength. Rolph nearly wept in relief, briefly wondering if dinosaurs *could* cry, but threw the useless musing away.

His rage abated slightly, and with it some of his height. "No...no no no," he tried to say, but it came out as a mess of hisses. He stabilized a head shorter than he had been, and a cold ball of anxiety dropped into his stomach. The giant looked from Rolph to Gertrude, considering which was more of a threat. For his part, Rolph scratched his feet against the moss, flinging his own share of nymphs into the air, and settled in a predatory crouch to await the assault.

Gertrude did her best to scrabble to her feet again, taking the opportunity afforded by Rolph's distraction. In the blink of a dinosaur's eye, the Giganotosaurus stood flanked by the two of them. The tables hadn't turned, not by a long shot to Rolph's mind, but perhaps they stood a better chance than they did before his metamorphosis. Gertrude bellowed a challenge and Rolph echoed it, further deepening the larger predator's indecision plain on her face. She stamped uncomfortably, scanning back and forth between them.

Rolph's chest erupted in pain as a new green beam struck him, a second lancing into Gertrude's skin as well. Apparently, he had been right, and he cursed internally as Karvalak's magic poured acid across his scales. The kobold's magic was more powerful than it had seemed from his vantage before and the spell was debilitating. He curled in on himself, mind afire with agony.

The kobold's shrill voice rose in another cackle. "Pathetic, druid! You think copying my friend here will save you?"

"NO, BUT THIS MIGHT!" a familiar voice cried.

Rolph opened eyes which had been shut in pain to witness something he had never expected in this lifetime. Eliard galloped at full speed astride Trike, long spear at the ready, trained on the monster's torso. The lance impacted her scales with an audible thud, then rammed through, the momentum carrying it deep into her stomach. The beast screeched and reared back, throwing Karvalak from his saddle. Eliard left his weapon embedded in the enormous creature, wheeling Trike around in a long arc until he faced the enemy again.

Karvalak hovered dazed in the air, suspended by magic. The giant dinosaur pawed ineffectively at her wound, snapping the wooden shaft of the spear, but leaving more than half the weapon lodged in her flesh. Rolph took a blast of energy to the side of his skull, hurled from Karvalak as he recovered his wits, but no new acidic attacks followed.

The attack rocked his head back and Rolph's vision fuzzed. He twisted in on himself and in a heartbeat, he had shrunk down to normal size, retaining his lizard-like features. In another breath his body reverted to its original form, leaving him gasping. He hastily dodged another burst.

"Rolph! His staff!" Eliard screamed, pointing at a spot on the ground not far from the young mason.

Trike and Gertrude circled the Giganotosaurus, occupying it, so Rolph bolted for where Eliard had indicated. Karvalak yelled and began his descent, but Rolph was quicker. He managed to snatch the twisted root from the ground before the kobold could land.

As soon as his hand came in contact with the staff, it started to glow. Unlike Fern's staff, which had been no more use to him than a walking stick, Karvalak's staff responded to his touch. In an instant, he sensed the natural magic pulsing within it and turned it on the kobold. The small creature didn't cower but drew power into his clawed hands, clearly ready to battle Rolph to the death.

Rolph raised the staff high in the air, a blue nimbus coalescing at the head. "It doesn't have to be this way. We only want to go home."

"You will *never* leave this place alive," Karvalak hissed.

Rolph sighed and gave a mental command to the staff, heavy with power in his hands. "Have it your way."

The cobalt beam struck the kobold before he could quip a reply, encasing him in ice. Rolph strode toward the creature as its skin blued and frosted, pouring every ounce of energy he could into this final attack.

Trike thundered past them to harry the larger dinosaur, striking at it with his horns and tearing at its flesh. Gertrude roared and darted in to nip at its limbs, forcing it back toward its den. Rolph stood witness as they corralled the creature, giving it a path to retreat. At first, it seemed like the beast might have taken Karvalak's path and fought to the end. As blood streamed from her wounded gut and she amassed more injuries, she appeared to change her mind. One last plaintive roar erupted from her blood-stained mouth before she turned tail and limped to the safety of her cave, disappearing into the darkness.

Rolph turned to survey his handiwork, and the bright eyes of the kobold stared back at him from the icy statue he had become. He threw the staff aside and hefted his hammer instead. Karvalak's fear-filled eyes, the only part of him that could still move, tracked his movements. The mason considered his options but in his heart he knew there was only one choice.

"I would have let you live, you know," he said.

The frozen statue said nothing, which dampened Rolph's grim satisfaction as he brought the hammer down in one swift motion, shattering the kobold into a million fragments.

Chapter Thirty-One

LOOTING THE ROOM

Rolph spent a few breaths standing still, letting the gravity of their success wash over him. It didn't feel real, being here at the end. Was this it? Was this the end? How was he alive?

A hand on his shoulder jolted him from his musings. Eliard.

He turned and clasped the cleric's forearm. "Happy to see you."

"Thought you might be." Eliard gave him a lopsided grin.

"Brought a friend, too, I see." Rolph nodded to Trike, who was nudging Gertrude's side, presumably looking over her wounds.

Eliard shrugged. "Figured you wouldn't mind the extra guest at your party. So, made it to the end of level ninety-five," he preened. "What are you going to do now?"

Rolph cracked a half smile. "I'll take an ale and a nap, thanks," he joked, and was rewarded with the cleric's scoff. He looked around. Now that his mind wasn't weighed down by the fumes he'd encountered when he'd entered the room, he was better able to take in his surroundings. Without the other druid's magic, the room was less fantastic than it had been. The subterranean flora was still there, but plain and dull as the rest of the Labyrinth without the surreal lens added by the poison.

He let his feet wander to the tree where he had first encountered Karvalak. If Gertrude had lived several lives, would the kobold return? Would the Labyrinth and the Triad cycle his life back to this place? How many times did every monster have to die? It sounded like an exhausting experience.

A flash of metal caught his eye. Rolph frowned and knelt, digging through the undergrowth until he uncovered the large, shining gold-colored chest.

"Loot!" Eliard exclaimed, startling Rolph. He hadn't noticed the man following him. The cleric stepped forward and tried to pry the lid open.

Rolph's heart sank, and the weariness of the day threatened to finally overwhelm him. "So, this is why you came back?"

Eliard stopped pawing at the chest and turned to Rolph with a chagrined look on his face. "No...I just...I'm sorry, Rolph." The sincerity of Eliard's voice caught Rolph off guard, and it was nothing like the syrupy sweetness of the doppelganger's apology. "I stood in front of the portal for a day, hemming and hawing about leaving. By the time I decided to stay, I had a hell of a time tracking you. We had to backtrack around a huge cage, too."

Rolph laughed, considering his first encounter with his "father". "That still doesn't tell me *why*, if it's not for gold."

Eliard rubbed the back of his head in discomfort. "Maiden's tears, Rolph, it's complicated! I thought about my family, and the man I promised them I'd be. Then I thought about your oath to Gertrude..."

Rolph nodded, waiting.

With a sigh, Eliard stumbled over his next words. "I didn't think I could look them in the eyes if I left you behind."

The pair stared at each other in silence for a long minute, until Eliard turned away and attempted to open the chest again.

"Looks like it needs a key," Rolph cleared his throat and muttered when the man grunted without success. A thought came to mind, and he returned to what had been the battlefield. Where

Karvalak's shattered pieces lay, there was a brass key hung around his neck, tucked into the folds in his robe.

He returned and passed the key over to Eliard. "You should probably have the honor."

"Of course I do," Eliard countered. "I saved your butt."

"Arrogant jerk," Rolph grumbled, but he didn't mean it. Eliard was right. He *had* saved them. And Rolph was grateful to him for it.

The key turned easily in the lock, and the lid of the chest popped open.

Eliard's excitement was not a silent affair, as he whooped and began giddily pulling jewels from the container.

Like a kid in a candy shop, Rolph thought to himself with amusement.

Eliard began sorting through the mass, tossing items he thought wouldn't catch a fair price over his shoulder and onto the ground.

A few rings, a bundle of potions wrapped in oilcloth, a pair of old boots with a toe worn through. Rolph turned his gaze to the dinosaurs, his interest waning, when a thud caught his attention. An amulet Eliard had tossed in the throw-away pile was heavier than the other jewelry the cleric had decided against. Curious, Rolph bent, picked it up, and examined the grooves of the engraving with the pad of his thumb. He didn't recognize the swirls in the metal, but it was pretty. He tucked it into his pocket. Eliard could have the rest of it, if he wanted it. Rolph was allowed at least one bauble from his adventure.

He paced over to Gertrude who was pushing Trike off of her and growling at him.

She snorted at Rolph and gestured with her neck at her cousin. The mason knew exactly what she was asking.

"Go on, leave her alone," he said to the triceratops. "She says she's fine, she means it."

Trike bent his head, chastised, and trundled away.

Gertrude let out an indignant huff of air in his direction as he left and turned a thankful glance down at her human.

"Looks like we made it, Gertie," Rolph lifted his arm to her neck as she bent down to be at eye-level with him. She purred her agreement deep in her throat, her eyes closing tiredly as she leaned into his hand. "I think we're ready to get out of here."

As if it had heard them, the door at the side of the room glowed blue.

Eliard looked up from his treasure gathering. He had closed the lid of the chest and wrapped it in spare rope, hefting the box onto his back like a pack. "Alright, folks. Let's give this a shot." Trike bayed sadly at him and Eliard waved him away. "No hard feelings, fella, but I'm not like Rolph. I'm not taking you with me."

Dejected, Trike hung his head and turned, leaving them. Gertrude grunted her approval, and Rolph couldn't help but feel bad for the dinosaur. Maybe he would always be a softie.

"Ready?" Eliard called.

Rolph had never been more ready for anything in his life. He and Gertrude joined Eliard at the door.

While Eliard went to stand near the gate, Rolph risked a look back at the room. This was the last time he would step into the Labyrinth. He was relieved to be going home but knew a part of him would be left here, in the caverns deep beneath the surface.

"Alright," Eliard said, drawing Rolph's gaze again. "Ladies first?"

Rolph shook his head. "No. You go, in case we can't get leave."

"Come on, Rolph. I came back so we could all go together."

"I know." Rolph clapped the taller man on the shoulder. "And you made it possible for us to even try. But I don't want you to feel obligated to stay, if Gertrude can't use the portal."

"But—"

"Go home to your family, Eliard," Rolph interrupted with a firm but kind tone.

The cleric opened his mouth to object, but Gertrude seemed to have sensed what was going on and leaned over to snort a hot breath into Eliard's face before he could reply.

Eliard raised his hands in surrender. "I can take a hint." He turned and stepped toward the portal but faltered. The man spun, grabbed Rolph in a bear hug, then let him go abruptly and dashed through the glowing field. That left Rolph standing bemused, staring at the cerulean expanse. He chuckled, shook his head, and then turned to Gertrude.

He cast the last of his magic, activating his communication spell. "Your turn."

"TOGETHER, TINY DINOSAUR."

Rolph frowned at the large creature. "I don't want the portal taking me and leaving you behind. If you can't make it, then I stay, and we find another way out."

"THERE IS NO OTHER—"

"We *find another way out*." Rolph stared down the dinosaur, which was something he never expected to do in his life. Gertrude snorted but bent her head in a show of gratitude.

She stepped forward and stood before the portal, deep breaths puffing out her chest. Rolph knew a case of nerves when he saw one.

"Go on. Let's go home."

"HOME..."

Rolph held his breath as she reached out and touched the shimmering gate.

EPILOGUE
THE TAIL OF THE MATTER

"I BET YOU'RE WONDERING whether it worked." Eliard leaned back and took a long pull of his tankard, finishing his ale. It was his fourth that night, happily paid for by this party of delvers as he wove his tale.

Lanterns burned fitfully on the wall of The Crone's Rest, one of the largest taverns in Wyrmwood. It was miles from Mayfair, but a popular stop on the way to the Labyrinth for those looking to challenge the goddesses. Wide wooden tables dotted the room, each big enough to accommodate a decently sized group. Sawdust littered the floor to soak up spilled beer, or other less fortunate fluids. Eliard enjoyed the atmosphere for what it was, rough and tumble. It reminded him of why he had gotten into delving in the beginning.

The place was popular with the adventuring crowd for many reasons. Some met to form alliances, swap gear, or trade stories about their time in the Labyrinth. Others came to listen to the old greybeards, the few who survived the mazes long enough to age properly, spin yarns for the younger folk.

Eliard was in between. Not too old, nor too young, but he had a *story* to tell, and five rapt faces stared at him, hanging on his every word. A dwarf, an elf, one gnome, and two humans rounded out this group. It wouldn't do to keep them in suspense for too long, otherwise he might not get a fifth drink out of them.

"C'mon, Eliard. Tell us what happened," whined the gnome, whose name Eliard had already forgotten.

The grin on Eliard's face broadened. He knew he had them in the palm of his hand. It wasn't the first time he'd told this tale, and by now he knew how to wring every last drop out of it.

"The part about the evil kobold?" Eliard asked.

"No!" the group cried in unison.

"You already told us that part, you drunk," complained the human called…Orien? Was that his name? He barely had hair on his chin, despite being this party's leader.

They get younger every year, Eliard thought, and sighed heavily.

"The dinosaur! Did Rolph and Gertrude get out?" asked the elf, who sipped at a glass of the inn's cheapest red wine.

"Hm. My throat is a bit parched after all that talking…"

Orien rolled his eyes and slapped his hand on the table. "Mother's tears, someone go get him another ale before I die of old age."

The dwarf, who had finished his own tankard, stood from the bench and sauntered to the bar for two refills. Eliard waited, eyes half-lidded, with a contented smile on his face. The rest of the party grumbled but devolved into small talk among themselves until the dwarf returned and set a new mug down in front of the cleric.

"Gently, now." Eliard grimaced as foam sloshed off the top and rescued the vessel before it could spill too much of its contents. He took a long swallow, savoring the bitter edge of the brew. "Now, where was I?"

A chorus of groans was the only response he received.

"Oh, yes, Rolph and Gertie. Well." Eliard placed his hands on the tabletop and leaned forward conspiratorially. The group settled in around him and mirrored his posture. Eliard's voice was low. Not quite a whisper, because on a busy night like this it would have been impossible to hear over the din of the crowd. Just low enough for a touch of dramatics. "I popped out of the entrance to the Labyrinth, like anyone who asks for the Triad's blessing to leave their domain. Except, I was alone."

"No!" yelled the human who wasn't named Orien. She tossed a copper at the dwarf, who she'd apparently had a bet with about whether Rolph would make good on his promise to the dinosaur.

"I was heartbroken and waited for a full day and night hoping they would come through. Maybe something had delayed them, rather than a complete failure after all the pain and struggle."

More than one party member had tears in their eyes. A shimmering wetness covered Eliard's as well.

"They say," he continued after a reasonably long moment of silence, "he still wanders the ninety-fifth level to this day, searching for another way to free Gertrude from her imprisonment at the hands of the Triad."

"How long has it been since you left?"

"Has anyone seen him since?"

"You've got to be out of your mind if you think I'm believing one word of this nonsense."

"We bought him five ales, for that?"

And on the commentary went, spilling from the mouths around the table.

Eliard waited patiently until they slowed and eventually stopped the rapid-fire questioning. He cleared his throat. "It's been ten long years since I last saw him. A few bold delvers have made it as far as the ninety-fifth level, and those who survived have said they caught occasional glimpses or heard the roar of a large reptilian predator. No one's spoken to him, but it's enough to convince me he's still trying."

"Why didn't you stay?" Orien asked with a voice full of skepticism.

"You mean, why did I abandon my friend again? After all I did to rescue him in his moment of greatest need?"

A wave of nods traveled around the table.

"I offered to stay," Eliard said, regret evident in his tone. "But Rolph insisted I go, to return to my family. He had nothing waiting for him out here. I didn't want to leave him but, by the Mother, I wanted to see my wife and kids again. So, I told him I'd look after the shop while he was gone and tell his parents he loved them."

The elf, who sat next to him, rested a hand on his shoulder. He patted it twice, accepting the sympathy.

"Speaking of the shop," Eliard said, slapping his thighs and standing abruptly. "I should get going. It's why I'm in town, after all, visiting your new quarryman. Lots of orders to fill." He drained his mug, turning it over and resting it back on the table. "Much obliged for the drinks."

With that, he took his leave, walking out of the tavern door without looking back. He walked down the street until he stood in front of a different shop. This one was a small office representing a quarry outside of Wyrmwood, rich in expensive stone.

His story was true, at least in part. He had taken up the hammer and learned some basic stonework after getting back and had been taking care of the store as he told the adventurers in the tavern. This venture outside of Mayfair was dropping in on a new investment, only a year old or so, funded from some of the spoils of his travels in the Labyrinth.

Eliard leaned against the brick facade, cool air from the alley next to him playing with the tassels on his shirt. The gentle breeze soon died, and a warmer steam replaced it.

"Do you ever get tired of telling the story?" Rolph asked, his voice echoing strangely from the alley.

Eliard took a half-chicken he had wrapped in a napkin and held it high in one hand. The hot breath intensified as a large reptilian nose snuffled at it, then collected the morsel with a gentle tongue. It barely crunched as Gertrude made quick work of the snack. He peered around the corner, and the dinosaur filled the wide alleyway with Rolph standing dwarfed at her feet.

"Never," Eliard said, chuckling. "The free drinks don't hurt, I'll tell you that much."

When they had finally made their way out of the Labyrinth, the shop had a foreclosure sign nailed to the door. Rolph had decided he didn't much like being a shop owner, and the debts he owed would be wiped out if the town thought he was dead. So, after a quick and private correspondence with Rolph's parents, to reassure them their son was not in fact dead, Eliard bought the place at auction for a pittance.

Rolph's debts were wiped clean, and he moved to a wooded glade outside of Wyrmwood. He lived a fairly private life for a year before re-entering society under an assumed name and establishing the quarry. No one needed to know the slabs were carted about by a T-Rex.

"Why do you have to exaggerate so much?" Rolph complained, patting Gertrude on the leg as she licked her lips clean. "Sure, most of it happened that way, but it's only been a couple of years."

"Well, they won't buy me as many drinks if the story is *boring*, Rolph." Eliard laughed. "Besides, that's how you become a *legend*."

ACKNOWLEDGEMENTS

THE ACKNOWLEDGEMENTS PAGE IS a place to say thank you to anyone or anything who has helped make the book possible. Being a part of the back matter, authors will often use acknowledgements to recognize a number of sources, or offer more detail about why the source is being recognized.

Or something, something. That's what they told me, anyways.

I want to acknowledge Inkfort Press for the opportunity to kill myself the past three months. As some variation of millennial living in today's modern era, any opportunity for a family friendly flavor of masochism is greatly appreciated.

I also want to thank my potentially non-existent pets, for listening to me and lending their fair judgement as I acted out fight-scenes and snippy lines of dialogue. Whether they are dogs, cats, fish, or a kobold on a leash—may your imagination serve you well.

I want to sincerely express gratitude to the editor of Underleveled. They also exist. They are in my body, we share skin. Please help, the voices are so loud.

And to that teacher that one time that said I would never make it. You *are* in fact, correct. I didn't want to succeed in NCAA sports anyways, so... joke's on you.

Made in the USA
Coppell, TX
30 December 2025